I0571716

Lady Eleanor's Christmas

Lady Eleanor Mysteries, Volume 3

Becca St. John

Published by Winterbourne Farm Publishing, LLC, 2018.

This is a work of fiction. Similarities to real people, places, or events are entirely coincidental.

LADY ELEANOR'S CHRISTMAS

First edition. October 17, 2018.

Copyright © 2018 Becca St. John.

ISBN: 978-0-9978902-7-3

Written by Becca St. John.

Thank you, Shiela Thomas, for reminding me that Christmas is all about the miracles

Chapter 1 ~ The Clock Strikes

23 rd December 1778 ~
If any room deserved haunting, it was this one.

Lady Eleanor grabbed a lap-rug and gave it a hardy shake. Years of dust billowed, swirling in the bitter drafts. She sneezed and gave it another snap.

St. Martins Hall, home to the Duke of Summerton, was in a terrible state. She'd known as much, thought herself prepared, explored to assess the depths of the matter. Though threadbare, her bedchamber and the salons were clean. Despite only a few mounts in the stables, empty stalls were freshly whitewashed. Nothing quite as bad as expected until she yanked aside the heavy library drapes.

Windows, tall as the two-story bookcases surrounding them, were too warped and twisted to bar the elements. Vines crept inside, hiding most of the leaded-glass panes. Where it could, gloomy light filtered through grimy frost, casting shadows over shelves of crumbling books and teetering towers of rare collections.

This magnificent library, overflowing with treasures, left to decay. Appalling neglect Eleanor would address the moment she married.

For now, she tucked the moth-eaten throw about her legs, nestled into the corner of a wingback chair, and pulled a heavy tome onto her lap. A hearty blow into fists warmed away stiffness. A quick brush of her hands dislodged any grime. Practical actions until she turned to the book in her lap.

Brusqueness became butterfly caresses, light, trembling as she explored the worn and cracked leather cover, traced the once gold title, now a series of raised lines. A book she'd heard of, more rumor than reality, yet here it was in her lap.

Before awe stopped her, she slipped fingers between vellum pages opening wide to the center revealing a Renaissance illustration of a dissected human body.

By her side lay a pamphlet on the applications of poisons along with a dissertation on identifying wounds. Beneath them a treatise on the decomposition of decaying flesh.

Heaven.

In all her years assisting Papa with affairs of law, determining innocence and guilt, they had never dealt with murder. Yet murder happened, often undetected. Eleanor would be ready. This library alone reason enough to marry the Duke's son, Lord Whittington. Not that she would marry for a library. There were other factors to consider but his father, and her own papa, wished it. So would her prospective groom.

In the stable lad's vernacular, the Summerton line didn't have a pot to piss in. Except, yes, with all their entailed properties and grand homes, they had multiple pots of that nature. However, should one break, they lacked the resources to replace it.

Not so her papa. Through a series of other's misfortunes, he rose from impoverished second cousin of a wealthy earl, to become the Earl. One day Eleanor was a spinster of two and twenty, the next a marital prize. Her resources would ensure refurbishment of all pisspots as well as walls and floors and tenants' homes... and libraries. Eleanor rather liked the idea of managing the endeavor.

She and Whittington would make a good match of it.

And she liked him, always had. When Papa had been his tutor, Whittington asked Eleanor to join him in the classroom. He'd meant to divide papa's attention, but any boy astute enough to recognize her hunger and ability to learn, was a precious friend.

She accepted his desire for society. He respected her need to study.

Which, unfortunately, would have to wait. Apparently, an unused library was a poor hiding place during a Christmas party.

Raucous merriment grew louder as it filtered through the closed door. Stuffing her precious finds under the blanket, she snatched up a discarded book, blew off the dust, barely cracking the spine before the door burst wide.

"Ho! We've found her," Whittington called out, as if the others hadn't flocked into the room, surrounding him like the halo of some golden god.

"What are you reading, Lady Eleanor?" he bent over, inspecting the cover. "A novel?" His eyebrow rose.

"I do read novels," she sniffed, thankful she'd managed to grab it right-side-up, hoping he wouldn't ask what it was about.

"Interesting," he nodded, a little too relieved.

He would be curious about her reading material.

He should be, she reminded herself, stamping down irritation. This was Whittington, not a sarcastic peacock who enjoyed ridicule. They may not have seen each other since childhood, but she was as fond of him now as she was then. Like her sister, Theo, he enjoyed people, saw the best in them. Perfectly delightful antidote to Eleanor's own dry skepticism.

Even now, in the gloomy confines of the study, Whittington' eyes sparkled. And there was the 'god' thing. People liked him, enjoyed following him. Natural selection or leadership instilled in a future duke? It didn't matter. Eleanor was content to be his duchess, for her own, singular reasons.

"We've come to drag you away," Whittington beamed with the promise of adventure, "to find mistletoe, ivy and boughs aplenty while we search for a yule log!"

Jolly cheers echoed down the long library, reminder that this would be a boisterous endeavor. No matter. She should put forth the effort. It was Christmas after all, time for festivities. She would have fun.

She truly would.

"Come with us," Whittington reached out, to help her stand.

"Oh, do!" Miss Giles, one of the guests, declared, "We are going to the haunted woods!"

Eleanor blinked and turned to Whittington, "You have a haunted wood?"

Lord Sudworth, a cousin of some sort to Whittington, leaned in, dripping with sepulcher menace, "Haunted with a monster that steps out of the mist, ax in hand, as a child, long gone from this world, wails."

"They don't always cry. Sometimes they laugh," Miss Giles gushed, with ghoulish awe.

"Goodness," Eleanor ignored the rush of conversation, musing on the possibility of a haunted wood. What kernel of truth created the legend and kept it alive? No matter how outlandish a fear, truth always lay at the bottom of it.

Before she could quiz anyone, Whittington offered his hand, "Please."

Back to the present in a blink, she placed her hand in his, and rose, "Thank you, m'lord."

He scowled, chaffing her hand, looking at the empty grate. "You should have had the fire lit."

Eleanor respected frugality. Until a few years ago, she'd had to. She also understood an unlit fire, in a room seldom used, was one thing. An empty grate, and need of a wife with deep pockets, told another. They were rationing coal, or wood, or both.

"There were so many books," she gestured to the library walls, smiling at the others, expecting them all to nod in understanding of her distraction.

Her audience leant forward, waiting, as if more needed to be said. For the life of her, she couldn't figure out what that was, so added. "I will have it lit now."

"Not necessary," Whittington claimed, "all you need are gloves and your cape." He released her hand.

"Oh, bother, I wasn't thinking," she couldn't accompany them, even if she'd wanted to, "Papa and Theo will be arriving shortly. I should be here to greet them."

"Surely they don't expect you to give up your entertainments," he tsked, "a footman can find us when they arrive."

"Perhaps," she hesitated, glanced back. A book corner visible from under the throw.

"To please me, Lady Eleanor," his childishly hopeful smile, so like her Theo's would be, charmed her beyond resistance.

The books, and her family, would be there when she returned, "Let me get my wrap."

"You see!" he turned to the others, "She will be joining us. Off you all go, wraps and gloves and ghostly weapons. A prize for the first to return to the entrance hall!"

A flurry of swirling skirts, and pivoting shoulders left Eleanor and Whittington alone in the cold library.

"A prize?" Eleanor placed her hand upon Whittington's gold embroidered jacket sleeve, arm held just far enough away he could walk without brushing or crushing her panniers.

"We've yet to name a Lord of Misrule!"

"You wouldn't!"

He waggled his brows like a Punch and Judy villain, "Wouldn't I?" Making her laugh.

She admired his ability to tease and have fun, even at his own expense, which impressed her more than his lion like looks. With every encounter, Eleanor warmed to his goodness.

"I'm sorry the fire wasn't prepared, or lit," he allowed her to proceed him past the jut of the staircase balustrade.

"I hadn't noticed." She lied, sidling around him, sorry she'd worn the wide hoops. Such a ridiculous fashion.

They stood at the foot of the stairs, footmen hurrying past. Grimms, the butler, managing a head bow as he stepped swiftly by.

"You don't mind?" Whittington asked, "All of us stealing you from your time alone?"

"How could I mind?" she squeezed his arm, touched that he understood her need for quiet. "I've never explored a haunted wood."

Not that ghosts existed.

Whittington shivered, comically, as a burst of real cold hit them.

Two footmen held the double entrance doors wide, Grimms the butler, silhouetted in the center, the jangle of coach bells announcing a new arrival.

"Oh, my! That must be Papa and Theo! They're here!" Eleanor cried, hurrying to the doorway as if it had been an age and not a week since she'd last seen them, "It's Papa's carriage!"

Holding her skirts, lest she fall, Eleanor ran down the stairs. Her father, Lord Bayford stepping down first, turning to help his younger daughter alight.

"Oh, E!" The moment Theo's feet touched the ground, a whirl of exclamations and wide gestures, she charged for Eleanor, "What a time we've had of it! You would have been fascinated!"

Their Theo. May she never change. Eleanor reached out to her sister, laughing at the sheer exuberance. The girl swooped in and clasped Eleanor's hands, her blue eyes wide, her looks and manner as light and delicate as Eleanor's were dark and sturdy.

"Robbers!" Theo declared.

"What?"

Eleanor looked to her father, who was frowning at Lord Whittington who, she realized, was staring at Theo. Oh, lord, to see his face. Theo must have come as quite a shock. The sniveling young brat, who had refused to leave his side even for a moment, had become a vibrant and beautiful young woman. Fighting a quiver of laughter, Eleanor managed serene introductions, "Yes, Lord Whittington, this is Theo, Lady Theodora. Perhaps you remember her?"

"Of course he knows it's me," Theo did laugh, almost shy, which Theo never was, "Lord Whittington," she curtseyed, and backed away, pulling Eleanor with her.

"Oh, my," she whispered to her sister, casting another quick peek at Whittington.

"Behave yourself, Theo," Eleanor teased, "what of this robbery?"

"Oh!" Theo burst, as if she'd completely forgotten, "E, do you believe it?" She whispered, "Father's friend, Sir Francis, was exquisite, pulling out a firearm, barking commands. I could have swooned."

To his credit, Whittington recovered his wits far more quickly than most young men. "We'll send men out. Where was this?"

"No," Bayford shook his head, "they are sorted. Coachman was excellent. Ex-soldier. He knew a thing or two. Sir Francis stayed behind, to deal with the matter. Magistrate you know. I must thank you for including him. Alone, for the holidays, we couldn't have that. He was to Christmas with us and I hated leaving him to his own devices."

"Of course, of course," Whittington assured, "Our pleasure."

"You would have loved it, E," Theo reiterated.

Too true. Eleanor rather fancied the idea of pointing a pistol at a brigand, though she refrained from admitting such unladylike aspirations. Perhaps she was learning what her ineptly absent chaperone, Lady Winifred, instructed. Eleanor should observe Theo. Apparently, despite her youth, Theo was the epitome of womanhood.

"What did you do?" Eleanor asked her.

"Why I..." Theo blinked, "I trembled!" she admitted. "Otherwise I would have been a nuisance. Especially if I'd fainted. That would have been a terrible distraction."

"Well done," Whittington applauded, "now let's get you out of the cold." He led the way up the stairs and into the hall.

Eleanor would have grabbed one of the pistols from beneath the carriage seat. No doubt, earning censure rather than applause.

"My apologies, Lord Bayford," he was saying to her father, "but the Duke is suffering with the gout. I'm afraid he's confined to his rooms. Perhaps you will visit him later?"

"Of course," Bayford agreed, as a footman took his travel cape.

"Perhaps, before you visit my father, you'd care to stretch your legs? A few of the guests have chosen a hunt for holly, mistletoe and yule log." Whittington explained, "We are happy to wait, if you'd like to join us."

"No, no," Bayford said, "Need to shake the dust off."

"Please, Father," Theo piped up, "I'd like to go. The fresh air would be welcomed."

Bayford scowled, displeased at her plea.

"I can tell you all about the robbers!" Theo promised Whittington.

"Lord Bayford?" Whittington asked.

"No," The older man patted his coat, no doubt looking for his pipe, "She had enough air in the carriage, and I need one of my gals here, to help me get settled. What do you say, Theo?"

Theo turned sorrowful blue eyes to Eleanor, "I will stay."

Eleanor laughed. "You will survive, Theo. Lord Whittington has planned a surfeit of entertainments. You will not go wanting."

"We will add another diversion," Whittington declared, "After we dine, Lady Theodora, will you thrill us all with tales of a robbery thwarted?" He signaled for the housekeeper who'd been standing at the side, "Mrs. Grimms will help you get situated."

As soon as Eleanor and Theo were inside the chamber they were to share, Theo danced about the room cooing, "That's the man you're to marry?" she stopped and gushed, "Oh, E, he's beautiful."

"Even I noticed that." Eleanor laughed as Theo sighed, a huge dramatic sound.

Handsome and a duke. A man of consequence. The Summerton line mismanaged their resources, but a centuries old bloodline secured their place in society. However wealthy Lady Eleanor was, the title was too new to lend weight to their social standing. Her marriage would open a world of possibilities for her sister's future.

As good a reason for marriage as any other. She would adjust, surely she would. Social demands couldn't be that trying. Could they?

AS WAS ITS WONT IN December, the sky hung low and grey. Perfect foil for flashes of peacock blue and holly red. Quick little revelations when women lifted their cape hoods, or flicked the whimsically embroidered cape edges, revealing vivid silk linings.

Theirs was a merry group. Cavalier and jovial, the men led, their dyed ostrich plumes swooping down from tricorns, coloring the way. Tottering behind in delicate ankle boots the women followed. One young lady wore pattens, platforms that raised her dainty feet above the dirt. A precarious adventure on uneven ground.

A walk in the woods, Whittington had said. Eleanor strode along in knee high oiled boots, laced with sturdy leather cord. Not dissimilar to what the men wore. She'd left her embroidered wool cape for a simpler one lined with fur that had her blending with the gloom. No match for the sparkle of beauty around her.

Lord Whittington didn't seem to mind. He'd nodded approvingly when they met at the bottom of the grand staircase.

"Ready to jump in and help," he'd said, and they'd laughed. They wouldn't sully themselves with physical labor. In search of yule log, holly and boughs of evergreens, the merrymakers would point and the servants would gather. All to be hauled to sheds until the morrow.

Bad luck to bring greenery indoors before Christmas eve, so they said.

Convinced superstition had a foot in the practical, she turned this myth over. She'd sorted enough of them out, she should be able to fathom this one.

Bad luck to walk under a ladder? Perfectly logical, people drop things.

Bad things to happen if you sweep after dark? You can't see the dirt in the shadows.

Seven years bad luck for a broken a mirror? It took that long to raise the funds to buy a new one.

And so forth.

"The grounds-men have already found the mistletoe," Whittington told everyone. "We will count on you ladies to place it."

And why the luck of kissing under mistletoe? Eleanor mused as she noticed Miss Giles glancing up through her lashes, at Whittington. He winked, playfully, as an older brother might wink at a young sister. The girl's cold pinkened cheeks grew darker.

An unfortunate infatuation. Betrothal for Miss Giles was not the goal of this Christmas Party. Lady Eleanor's was.

Discreetly, Eleanor pulled off a glove, and brushed her cheek, as if something had landed on it.

No heat. Not even a hint of becoming blush when, moments ago, she'd imagined standing beneath the mistletoe with Lord Whittington. Fanciful daydream, but nothing to send blood to her cheeks.

She raised her hood against the deepening gloom as the church bell tolled over the land. One... two...

A child's cry rose in the soft mist, flushing squawks from the women as they pulled into a clutch, their hooded heads bobbing and shifting like a colorful horde of monks.

Three... four... the clock pealed.

Alert and still, the men's gazes swept the undergrowth, up into the trees, searching for the source of the cry even as it faded.

The chill running up her spine had everything to do with the cold. Eleanor shivered it away. An unhappy child was crying, somewhere, and the sound carried.

"It's the boy," Miss Giles' low maudlin whisper drew the women closer. "Listen, it's coming from the lake."

Someone whimpered.

"A boy, what boy?" Eleanor asked.

"The drowned child," Miss Giles lamented, "when they filled the lake."

"That was two years ago," Whittington snapped, brow furrowed, jaw rigid.

"What lake?" Eleanor asked, only to be ignored, all eyes on a groundsman running toward them, hands flailing.

"M'lord! M'lord! Come see what we've found!" he shouted.

"Nooooo," someone cried, "the body! And we've just heard him cry!"

"Don't be ridiculous," Lady Eleanor chastised, hoping to cut off ghoulish hysteria. "A dead child doesn't cry."

The hoods shifted, all the women staring at her, as if she were the one crazed.

"Well it doesn't," she said. Especially not after two years.

"Not a chil'" the servant said, "but somethin' of his."

"Ohhhs!" and "Nooos" and undefinable laments filled the air.

Only Eleanor stepped forward, "May I see?" she asked.

Wide eyed the servant looked from her to Whittington, who nodded assent, joining Lady Eleanor, the rest falling in behind.

"Who is this boy?" she asked.

"Child of Tom Baker," Whittington explained, "Tom's father was the baker from Lower Slough," he explained. "This lake is named for the son."

"Tom's Lake, or Baker's Lake?"

"Neither. Briden's Lake, for Tom's son."

"Briden? That's an unusual name for a village Baker." Eleanor noted.

With a shrug, Whittington said, "Could be from the mother's people. We don't know who they are."

"That is odd, when one is from a small village. Where is this lake?" she asked again.

Whittington stopped and turned her, standing behind, reaching around, so close she felt his breath on her face, his warmth surrounding her as he pointed. Following the line of his arm she saw it, amazed she hadn't realized sooner.

They'd taken a trail from the back of the house, through the woods, sloping down the whole way. Clearly seen through the branches, not twenty yards away, was the lake. In summer it would have been hidden entirely by foliage. In winter, the lake matched the grey of the sky. She'd not even realized it was there.

"The village, Lower Slough, used to be where the lake is," Whittington explained, straightening away, "until a few years ago, when Lord Grey claimed he needed a reservoir. Rumor has it, the village spoiled his view."

"Isn't that your estate?" Lady Eleanor asked, "What of the inhabitants?"

"Yes, in theory the Earls of Grey pledged fealty to my forefathers and my forefathers pledged fealty to the King. Very medieval. However, the line of the Earl of Grey died out about three generations ago."

"But you said Lord Grey flooded this area recently." Eleanor reminded him.

"Purchased." He raised his hand, foregoing the question of selling entailed property, "The land exchange was a complicated and unpleasant process dealing with ancient agreements. The man usurped a title, found a way to acquire the lands and brought it to Father. The only good thing to come of it was the purchase price and revenues in perpetuity. Father was almost pleased with that."

"Usurped?"

Disdain apparent, Whittington admitted, "Buying a title. Appalls Father to no end. Can't say I like it much either. The weight of ancestry does not come without burden. But there you have it. Father managed to sell the land to what he calls The Usurper."

"Is the man that bad?" Eleanor wondered.

"He flooded a village, quite possibly with an old woman and a child in it. He's that bad." "Oh, dear! And the inhabitants of Lower Slough?" she pressed.

"He built another village, one to his liking. That would be Greystone. Most were tenants and had no option but do what they were told. He provided the homes, they moved. See the ridge rising up from the opposite bank? Greystone is on the far side of it."

"The boy?"

The crying started again. Whittington stopped, cocking his head.

"It does sound as if it's coming from the lake," she agreed, "but I could swear he's saying something. Calling for something through his tears." She strained to hear but the groundsman was urging them forward so they gave it up and hurried along.

"M'lord, it's here." The man stood on the path, pointing to the water's edge. Whittington went first, but Lady Eleanor was not far behind, thankful for her sturdy boots.

They stood, looking down on a damp mass of scraggly fur.

"Excuse me," Stepping past Whittington, Lady Eleanor crouched down, grabbing a nearby stick to upend the sodden lump. Beady black button eyes stared back. A scraggly toy bear nestled in a tangle of weeds. For all its unkempt appearance, it had once been a prize. A well-stuffed rag doll of a bear, fashioned from curly sheep's fur. It was dressed in a long shirt, short, stand-up collar and three star-shaped buttons down an elaborately embroidered placket on the left of the chest. A most unusual toy for a wealthy family. Certainly not one for a villager.

The child's cry turned to a wail. One of the women started weeping. "He knows you're looking at his Buppa."

Whittington scowled and asked his friend, "Sudworth, take the women back. We're done looking for greenery."

"It's his toy, isn't it?" Miss Giles stepped forward, before anyone could pull her away.

"It could be anyone's," Whittington told her.

"It's his," another servant said, "whole county knowd about the bear. No one seen the likes 'afore. 'Cept we thought them buttons down the front twer moons."

"You are very familiar. Are you from the Earl's household?" she asked the man.

Shifting about, he twisted his forelock, "Yes m'am, until he flooded us out. Thens we came here."

"Your name?" she asked.

A quick glance at Whittington before he bent his head, murmuring, "Auggie, m'lady."

Eleanor studied him, noting the scar under his left eye. A helpful clue for recognizing him. "Very good." She dismissed him and picked up the toy, water streaming from it, "When was this lost?"

"When the dam were exploded and the floods drowned Lower Slough. The child and his nana..." Auggie said.

"Exploded? They used explosives?" Lady Eleanor muttered.

"That's enough, Auggie," Whittington said. "Lady Eleanor, shall we?" Stepping close, Whittington offered his arm.

"Please, keep back," she scowled, shooing him away, "when you reach the hall, ask my father to join me here."

"What do you want here?" Whittington asked, "It's just a toy. Nothing can be proven."

Drinking in the surroundings, she suggested, "A distinctive toy that doesn't belong here. That, in itself, raises questions," and looked up. "Did they ever find the child's body?"

"No," Whittington said, "but I'm surprised the bear made it to shore. Everything is well under water, has been for two years. They didn't stand a chance."

"Hmmm," she looked back at the ground as all but Whittington started to leave, no doubt bored by what looked to be no more than a sodden mess. But just as there was more to the story of the boy and his father, there was more to this bedraggled bear than a long-lost toy. "Am I to assume the dam was purposely opened when the child drowned?"

He looked away, then back, "There was an inquest, it did not go to trial. From what I understood it was a misunderstanding. The village was flooded a day ahead of schedule. A child and his nana drowned," he confirmed.

"Why hadn't they left? When the others abandoned the village, why just the two of them still there."

"I don't know," he said, but he did know, she could tell. His eyes shifted, unable to look at her straight on, as he'd been doing.

"No sign of them since?"

"None." He looked back to what was now an empty pathway except for three servants awaiting instruction before returning his gaze to Lady Eleanor, "Impossible to keep a secret in these villages. If they were alive, people would know."

Again, he made to step near. "Please, stay back," Eleanor warned.

He frowned.

She sighed, giving in to his reluctance, "My father would say that," she hedged, "or not, depending on his interest. Best we not interfere until he's had a chance to make that decision." Men respected idiosyncrasies within their own gender but question and over-ride them in a woman.

"The clock struck four earlier, it will be dark soon. Surely you want to return to the Hall."

"I will wait," she told him. "Father will think to bring lanterns."

He blinked, nonplussed. "There's nothing here but a toy. Sad as that is..." he kept glancing back, no doubt wanting to catch up with the others, "Surely you will join us for the festivities."

There was something here, a vague niggling. Not strong enough to divulge, but enough she wasn't ready to leave. "You go, I will be fine and will very much try to return in time."

He scrunched down, meeting her eye to eye, "I don't know what you expect to learn by staying out here, but if you feel it is necessary I will stay with you."

Touched, by his acceptance, she reached out, placing her hand on his arm. Not many men would be so understanding. "I will be fine," she told him, "Go back to the hall. My father will be here shortly. No reason for you to stay."

"It is cold," Lord Whittington needlessly reminded her, "shall we just take the..."

"In a moment." The light was fading. She hoped to catch what it was that troubled her before it was gone entirely. "After my father arrives. Now go before night settles completely. Leave Auggie here. He'll watch over me."

Clearly, Whittington struggled with his decision.

"I'm being a terrible guest, that does not mean you need be a terrible host." she shooed him away, laughing to keep it light, but very determined. "Go!"

"If you insist," he bowed, not at all at ease with her decision, and left.

The moment he was out of sight, she looked at Auggie. "What happened to Tom Baker?" Her question startled him. He looked away, back again, down at his boots.

"I'm very patient," she said.

"We don' rightly know," he admitted, "one day he was here, somefin' terrible weighing 'im down. The next he's gone."

"And the child?"

"The baby wert just a tot, barely from his mama's womb, left on the Baker's doorstep. There wert a note. Said Tom was in the navy and the boy wert his."

"How long after he left?" she asked.

Auggie looked away, lips scrunched tight.

"They're all gone now, aren't they? The whole of his family." Lady Eleanor guessed, "Who is it going to hurt for you to tell me?"

Nostrils flared, he looked at her, as if determining her worth, "My people are not for gossip. Devil's own language."

"This is not gossip," Eleanor explained, "there is something wrong here and I want to know what it is."

"Boy came 'bout seven months afa Tom left," Auggie admitted.

Eleanor rocked back on her heels, "Ah, I see."

No mention of marriage. No father or mother but a child given to grandparents. Left to die. Alone.

"Auggie," Eleanor said, urgent now, "that doesn't explain why they were alone in the village. Where was the baker and why hadn't they left?"

"Baker died but his wife kept the bakery goin' until the move," he spit, "Lord Grey offered the rent to someun' else, din' he. Din' wan' old lady Baker in the new 'un. Said she were too old."

"He didn't provide a new home for her?"

Auggie shook his head. "But she t'wernt worried, none. Said she'd seen her Tom and he were t' move her. Maybe he did, but we ne'r seen them from the flood to now."

Eleanor rose. "That's enough for today. I will fetch my father. We will return with lanterns, see what he sees."

"Yes, m'lady," Auggie said and led the way.

There was more to this little bear than it being a boy's long-lost toy.

Chapter 2 ~ It's Only a Toy

Already dressed for supper, Theo waited impatiently for Eleanor. Her sister was a bloodhound to crime. Good thing, too. Except this was just a toy. No one was injured or worse. If there was a crime it happened two years ago.

It could wait.

Except Eleanor couldn't. Of all nights for E to be distracted. Theo's first step out from under her governess' care, and no one to guide her.

How was she to navigate the staircase? Greetings in the salon?? She needed Eleanor or their father to take her arm. Show her the hows and whys of society. E had promised to be by her side. But she wasn't.

With a poof of skirts, Theo plonked down on the bed, keeping herself upright to avoid ruining her hair, built up as high as her face was long. She lifted her legs, gazing down at the dainty points of her shoes with their adorable little buckles, sparkling with tiny gems. She'd spent days and days agonizing over what she would wear on this first night of festivities.

Instead, she'd be stuck in this room waiting until dawn.

Her stomach growled.

"Bother!"

Someone rapped at the door.

"Enter," she called, prepared to hear that Eleanor was detained.

Unprepared for Lord Whittington to be standing there.

"I'd best not step inside, Lady Theodora, even with my cousin present."

Young Miss Alicia, all dangling gold curls and cupid face peered around her cousin.

"Oh, my goodness no!" Theo jackknifed off the bed, the weight of her tall hair nearly toppling her before she regained equilibrium and smoothed the fall of her skirts, discreetly settling her hoops, afraid they were uneven or tilting or...

"You look marvelous," Lord Whittington praised, "and would be sorely missed below stairs, if you weren't to attend supper."

"I was waiting for my sister."

"She's delayed," Alicia chimed in, pushing past Whittington, "with your father and the magistrate," she confirmed, "and your aunt is down with the megrims. I think she spent too much time sipping port with my uncle, who won't join us because of his gout."

"That's enough, Alicia, you'll frighten the girl off." Whittington admonished, explaining to Theo, "My cousin here insists we coerce you to join us, despite the absence of your family,"

"We've come to escort you to the salon." Alicia said for herself.

"Oh!" Theo squeaked, "I am ready." She wished she could peer in the reflecting glass, to see if she'd dislodged her curls, wrinkled her skirts, when she'd so foolishly flung herself onto the bed. She dare not with a gentleman present. He'd think her vain.

"Very good." He offered his arm, the lace of his cuff handsomely framing his wrist and dangling down, "they will be ringing for supper soon."

Theo stepped out of her room, her heart aflutter, shyly looking up at the man who would be her new brother-in-law.

Oh, joy!

This lovely, lovely man would be marrying her sister. Her father said it would be so, as did his father. It was just down to the couple, themselves.

Eleanor said it was going quite well. She expected all to be in order soon. Hopefully, it would all go smoothly. Her sister could be quite astute, but then there she was, late for supper over a silly toy. Her wild distractions and unfeminine interests could destroy everything.

Placing her hand on his arm Theo took a peek determined not to swoon. The man was top of the tree, a dashing gallant. Far too good for Eleanor to lose.

If Eleanor couldn't be there, Theo would accompany him everywhere, influence him to all that was wonderful about her sister. By the time she was done, there would be no question but he sweep Eleanor straight-up into marriage.

"Thank you, good sir," she said, feeling more confident as it was Eleanor she represented and not the scary prospect of presenting herself. "How very kind of you to fetch me."

THE SUN HAD SET HOURS ago, footprints frozen in the mud, reminders of the earlier tramplings. Nothing of any note, yet Eleanor couldn't quite stop looking.

"Haven't you seen enough?" Her father's rasp pulled her away. She'd kept him out too long. Hadn't given an ounce of consideration for his long journey. He'd barely had a rest before she summoned him to the bitter December night. And she knew how cold seeped into his bones and could settle into his chest. She should have thought.

"Nearly, Papa, I promise." She lowered the lantern to better see the ground.

They'd already gone back to the hall to question any servants who once lived in Lower Slough.

"We do not have any of Grey's people here, in the house," the butler informed them, "only one on the grounds and a couple lads in the stables."

They'd inquired at the stables, without success.

"'Aven' seen him, never did, afer he left," a groom told her.

"Before? Do you remember before he left?"

"Aye," he admitted, though he shook his head and turned away, done with the questioning. Leaving her with more questions.

"It's in your mind's eye," Sir Francis straightened from where he leaned against a tree, not helping at all when he was the magistrate in charge. "There are men we can call in to do this."

"Not as thoroughly." She snapped, "And what do you mean, 'it's in my mind's eye'?" She stood, her back aching from bending, taking advantage of the break to tuck her hands into the crease of her arms, warming them. The lantern sat on the ground, shining the light upward.

"You keep looking at the ground because there is something you've seen that isn't quite right, but you don't know what it is."

He did that all the time, challenged her, guiding in directions she either wasn't ready to take or plain out didn't want to take. It was exceedingly bothersome, that he could be so accurate, but she was not so small minded to begrudge his assessment. "I still don't know what it is."

"Stop looking. You've seen enough. It's there, it's teasing you. In the middle of the night you will sit up and gasp, 'I've got it!' and you will have," Sir Francis promised.

"Too true," her father admitted. "You've a fabulous memory, Eleanor. You'll be able to remember what you've been studying. No need to labor it to death."

She sniffled, wiggling her frozen nose, watching the fog of her sigh rise up to the sky. "I suppose you're right," she decided, slipping her arm into her father's, "and a fire would be quite welcome, don't you think?"

"Rest," Lord Bayford patted her hand, "we'll tuck in again tomorrow."

"I wish we could find the answers tonight."

"No doubt," Sir Francis agreed. He'd reached her other side, as they followed the servants with the lanterns. As though she weren't there, he reminded her father, "She always gets like this."

"Always," her father chuckled. "Once, when I'd thought she'd been tucked in her warm bed she was traipsing about to see what really caused the fairy lights in the lake."

"What did she find?" Sir Francis asked, though Eleanor suspected he'd heard this story before. Her father was quite fond of the telling. She stole his thunder.

"Gypsies, luring fish with lanterns," she said.

"But they weren't legal, were they E? We nearly had to pay a ransom to get you freed. Terrible time that was. Barely lived through it."

"Ha, they couldn't capture an old mare standing still," Eleanor snorted, "it was easy enough to get free of them."

Actually, it hadn't been. A terribly frightening time, indeed. Never again would she go into the woods alone at night. Never.

They'd reached the back of the hall.

"We should go in the servant's door," she said.

"Whatever for?" Sir Francis asked, "We are not servants!"

Eleanor glanced at the mud stains on her warm wrap, debris snagged in the fur cuffs. "I'm unkept..."

Chuckling, Sir Francis brushed a bit of dirt from her cheek.

She jerked away, "I will clean myself, thank you."

Which would have to wait until she made it to her rooms. Which was precisely why she wanted to go through the servants' area and up their stairs. "I will not go traipsing around St. Martins like this," Her skirts sagged at the sides as she'd discreetly removed the panniers before coming out again.

Sir Francis waylaid her as she headed for the servant's entrance. "They will not praise you for trespassing on their private space."

She jerked free, "I'm not trespassing, just passing through."

"Trespass," he said.

"Don't be ridiculous!" She argued and walked into the hall through the kitchen entrance.

The servants in the corridor froze, curtsied and froze again. Of course, Sir Francis would be correct. Every room they passed, the occupants would stop and stare.

"As long as we are here, shall we see if we can't sneak..." Sir Francis slipped down a side corridor and through a doorway.

What could he be thinking? He'd considered this a bad idea and yet now, off he goes, keeping them longer.

"Come on then, Eleanor," her father tugged her.

If nothing else, it was warm down here. Warmer than the rooms above stairs. They followed Sir Francis' path and stepped into a blast of heat, scent so heavenly her knees nearly buckled.

"Ahhhh," her father came up beside her, nose to the air, drawing in the sweet smell of honey, nuts and yeasty bread.

Trust Sir Francis to find the bakery and to be deep in counsel with, judging by the amount of flour he wore, the baker. A big man, who glanced toward the doorway and just as quickly away, but not so fast he could hide the massive scars covering his head and neck. Burn scars. An awful hazard for kitchen help.

The butler burst into the room, fighting for breath. Obviously, summoned to rid the kitchens of unwanted guests.

"Lord Whittington is entertaining in the music room. They have all dined." He informed them.

"Very good," Sir Francis said, as if he were in the library heading for the hallway. He did, in fact, make to leave the bakery, "We will go above stairs. Have trays sent to our rooms."

"Of course, Sir Francis," the butler said, "may I show you the way above stairs?"

"Thank you," Sir Francis responded, adding, "and some of those sweet rolls? Will you see they are on the tray?"

"As you wish."

Sir Francis did not react to Eleanor's scowl until they were free of the servants.

"Do you not want to eat?" he asked.

"Don't be ridiculous. Of course I want a meal," she retorted.

"Then why the glare?"

Because he'd usurped her position. She should have directed the butler, requested sustenance. It was imperative she present herself as the future lady of the house. Sir Francis undermined her intention. Unfortunately, an inescapable yawn waylaid her set-down.

"You've a right to be tired," he noted, "Your father and I will escort you above stairs?"

And so the sorry threesome dragged their tired feet as they made their way to their chambers above stairs. Sir Francis waited while her father bid her goodnight at her door.

"Don't forget to save time for Lord Whittington tomorrow."

"I shan't forget, father." She'd forgotten him, entirely, while they were outdoors. "Good night."

He kissed her cheek, "Whittington appears genuinely interested but best not push him too far."

"Are you saying I'm beyond control?"

"A bloodhound to the scent," Bayford chuckled.

Sir Francis had the gall to laugh.

"Tenacious," Eleanor allowed.

"Like a terrier?" Francis asked.

"Don't be ridiculous," she snapped and went into her chamber, shutting the door with a firm click. She'd half expected Theo to be sitting there fuming, having lost her opportunity to dine with the others.

But Theo wasn't there. She must have braved the walk on her own. Good for her.

Except she needed an escort. Perhaps Aunt Winifred had joined her. Which was worse. Far worse. Winifred had been in her cups in the afternoon. No telling what condition she was in tonight.

Poor Theo could be shrinking in embarrassment.

Except Theo wouldn't shrink. She would turn it into something delightful, or sorrowful or some such, so everyone felt something, and no one judged.

Eleanor sat on the counterpane, debating falling straight back and going to sleep or waiting for Theo to return, when a scratch on the door made the decision for her. Footmen, one with buckets of steaming water, another bearing a large tray laden with dome covered pates. Her maid, Gracie, hurried in, all a purpose.

"Water in there," she routed to the dressing room. "Pour it into the pitcher on the washstand, leave what's left, I will take care of it," as if the servants were clueless about their duties. "You," she directed the footman with the tray, "place that there, then move this table here, near the fire and pull that chair to it. You may lay the cloth and set the place for m'lady."

New to her post, and not so very far removed from a lower servant, Gracie instructed with uppity confidence. Eleanor didn't dare laugh. She knew Gracie's recent status change, the servants of St. Martins did not. Gracie was setting the tone just in case her charge became the next Countess of Whittington. Clever of her. Precisely why Eleanor chose her. She needed a maid who could think.

As the footmen left, Gracie placed a basin of water on the floor by the fire. "Let's get you out of those cold clothes and your feet into that water," she said, urging Eleanor stand still as she drew her clothes off. "Look at you, near as blue as the ice, and you had your father standing out there too."

"Horrid of me, I know," Eleanor lamented. Keeping her father out, forgetting about Theo at supper without her family.

"Yes, yes," Gracie nodded as she stripped Eleanor of her snow dampened bodice, "and everyone is full of whispers about you out there over a drowned toy bear."

Eleanor stopped Gracie from unfastening her skirts, "What did you say?"

"They wouldn't be sticking their noses up if you explained why you were looking," the girl nodded. "And what were you looking for?"

"I'm not certain yet," she admitted, "but I will know when I see it."

Gracie stripped away the last of her clothes and dropped a flannel night dress over her head.

"Well, that puts me in a bind," the maid admitted, nudging Eleanor to the wash basin, to put her hands in the warm water. Delicious warmth. She stood like that, splashing it on her face, submerging her hands until it started to cool. Drying off she caught her image in the looking glass. Cheeks and nose red, tangled hair, half up, half down. "Oh, my," she mourned. At least no one of importance had seen. Just her father, who wouldn't have noticed. The servants, who wouldn't have cared, and Sir Francis who didn't matter. He'd seen her amid investigations enough not to be shocked.

"Here now, let's get your feet into that tub. I've put salts in it, to draw the cold out," Gracie hurried ahead, to move the basin from the hearth to beneath the impromptu tablecloth. Eleanor took her seat, sighing with pleasure as she sank her feet into the warmth and nearly swooning at the plate of warm stew with thick slices of bread Gracie placed before her.

"Tell me what else they're saying below stairs," she said around bites.

Gracie tutted, arranging the damp clothes close to the heat of the fire, "It's not right to tell tales."

"You are my ears, Gracie," Eleanor explained, "Surely they're talking about the bear."

"Oh, well, that..." Gracie took her time, aligning the folds of the garment, "they're full of the ghosts, and how it were cryin' and the bear found."

"A servant said it was the boy's, he identified it."

"It was the boy's true enough," Gracie said, "a gift from Lady Grey."

"A gift from Lady Grey?" Eleanor marveled, "That is extraordinary, a whole quandary of its own, but it certainly explains how a villager's son came to have such a distinctive toy."

"Suppose so's?" Gracie murmured.

The fire crackled in the grate, the windows creaked with the force of the snow, that now came sideways at the house. They'd come in just in time.

The chamber door opened, and Theo slipped in, "Oh, E, you're back!" she ran across the room, crouching down, clasping her sister's hand. "You are the luckiest woman in the world!"

Startled, Eleanor pulled free, "How so?"

Theo blinked, "Why Lord Whittington, of course! He's divine!"

She'd forgotten Lord Whittington. Again. Oh bother. What was wrong with her? Handsome, fun, kind, he was not the sort a gal forgot! What a thoughtless woman she was. Too involved in her own interests.

"He was great fun when we were young," Eleanor explained, because Theo would have been too small to remember. At three and four years old, she'd clung to him as tenaciously as the baby blankie she'd carried. Perhaps she did remember. He'd been terribly indulgent, tossing her in the air, carrying her about on his shoulders. Another factor in his favor. He was a good man.

"Of course!" Theo exclaimed, "He's handsome and intelligent and the most thoughtful man I've ever encountered."

Eleanor put her hand over Theo's, willing to be pulled in by her exuberance.

"Papa did well, didn't he?" Eleanor asked, for it was her father who had arranged the introduction. There were other women, with grander funds than she. Women who were daughters of Earls from birth, not newcomers to both title and fortune.

"Well, the Duke and Father have been friends ever so long and the Duke considers you the best of the lot for his son!" Theo exclaimed, "and Father is no fool to turn that away."

"He's no fool." Eleanor had to agree.

Theo gushed, "I so hope he will find the perfect husband for me as well."

That was the crux. The reason Eleanor needed this match as much as Whittington needed her money. Theo's marriage prospects.

She would not leave Theo to be chaperoned by Aunt Winifred. Precisely why Eleanor had not gone to court in the first place. A young lady's reputation depended on a proper chaperone. Coming out under Aunt Winifred's inept tutelage would have been Eleanor's ruin.

Eleanor had no suitors. Would not have this one, if not for the fathers. Between her studies and investigations, she'd not been bothered. Theo was another matter. Society and marriage the center of all her dreams.

Dreams Eleanor could provide, as a married woman. Under the auspices of the Duke of Summerton, Eleanor would introduce to the highest throngs of society. Her sister's beauty and charm would do the rest. She would shine.

All Eleanor need do is marry a man she was fond of.

Not so difficult.

"You will delight in the court," Eleanor told her, "powerful men reduced to fisticuffs to gain access." She waggled her eyebrows.

"You should have gone," Theo reminded her.

Eleanor shrugged her shoulders, pulling her feet from the cooling pan of water, stopping her maid, "I can manage my own slippers, Gracie."

"But a lady is not supposed to, especially a duchess," Theo explained, "the Duchess of Devonshire is attended by six ladies when she undresses."

"Is she?" Lady Eleanor asked. "And here's our poor Gracie serving two of us. I suppose Gracie told you this, having heard it from the other servants."

"Miss Alicia told me," Theo gushed, "Lord Whittington's cousin. You must meet her, Eleanor. She's exceptional."

"Miss Alicia, or do you mean the Duchess of Devonshire?"

Theo threw a pillow, "You know the Duchess, E! That's Georgiana Spenser, you met her just before her marriage, when Papa became an earl."

She'd been betrothed, at sixteen. The age Theo approached.

"Then you mean Miss Alicia. I've met her as well," Eleanor said, "she's delightful. You will probably go to court together."

Whittington had yet to make a proclamation, but when Eleanor spoke of taking her sister to court he'd said, "Well then, why don't we sponsor your sister and my cousin together?"

"Wonderful!" Theo clasped her hands to her mouth.

"You do know, dearest, that your beauty and charm will have half the court after you."

"Only half?" Theo teased.

"The other half are women," Eleanor explained.

Theo snorted.

"You are quite beautiful," Eleanor told her, brushing her cheek, delicate as porcelain touched by a rose.

"You are beautiful too," Theo proclaimed, her loyalty stronger than honesty.

"Handsome," Eleanor corrected. Skin like a common white mug without the slightest hint of pink. "Not unattractive, but more... more..."

"Stately, like a duchess!"

Eleanor nodded, "Yes, I will accept that. Thank you." A duchess should be strong, regal. No harm in that. "And a very tired future duchess," she yawned.

Tomorrow, she would spend time with Lord Whittington, though it wasn't necessary. They would be married, and they would sponsor her sister and his cousin at court. He'd made his choice, or so his father confessed to her father.

She would agree to the match as well. Any man who stepped aside, allowing her to investigate a crime... incited by no more than a bedraggled toy bear... should not be discarded.

"You are so lucky," Theo said, sitting at the dressing table while Gracie pulled the pins from her hair, freeing the horsehair filler that framed its height, "He is such a gentleman."

"Yes," Eleanor agreed, "I am very lucky." And slipped into the other side of the bed, to dream of chasing villains, whose faces she couldn't see.

She did not dream of Lord Whittington.

Her sister did.

Chapter 3 ~ The Wrong Child

December 1778 ~
24 Just a toy, no more.

Sir Francis sat at the desk, tapping his fingers on a blank sheet of stationery before him. He'd already sent a note to Lord Bayford. No reason to be sitting there. Things to do, arrangements to make, questions to align.

Instead, he kept thinking about Bayford's eldest. Not a girl, a woman, set on marriage to a light-hearted gentleman. Except she wasn't light hearted. Lady Eleanor was serious, capable of catching the most obscure connections in the most ordinary of situations.

Like a sodden toy.

How had she known?

From the very first, she'd fascinated him. The way that mind of hers worked. Startling, catching a man unguarded. He'd come to depend on her busy, convoluted thinking. Her father would miss her. She ruled that household. Saw that everything was in order.

She'd make a fine duchess, when that day came. Whittington's father, the Duke, was an astute man to consider her over others.

A waste she'd not be practicing her skills after marriage. It wouldn't come easy, trading in a keen analytical mind for the dishonest delights of society.

Innuendo and deceit not her style. Organizing a household befits, but endless vacuous entertaining would drive her mad.

Absolutely no conversation on the natural sciences.

He sighed, placing the empty sheet on top of the stack of stationery.

No more investigations for her in her very near future. A shame.

Sir Francis rose, only to stand, fingers drumming the desk top.

No more adventures for that perceptive nose she had for wrongs and rights. Not after this Christmas. Not that it was his concern. Or his place to make her decisions by not offering invitations.

Why did he even hesitate? He never did before. Was it because her father was eager for the match? Would not approve of Francis distracting his daughter. All he mentioned in Bayford's note was one day's travel away from her prospective husband. That was all. What sort of man gave up a fortuitous alliance for one day's absence?

Perhaps Lord Bayford wasn't as worried about the prospective groom changing his mind as the bride changing hers.

Sitting, Sir Francis pulled a sheet of stationery onto the desk, dipped his quill into the ink and wrote.

Lady Eleanor,

At the risk of burdening you with a confidence that must not be revealed, Lord and Lady Grey have requested my presence with the utmost urgency. Your esteemed father will accompany me on this journey. Do you wish to attend?

We depart within the hour,

Your Servant,

Sir Francis

A terrier, he'd called her. Let her tug at that.

"ISN'T IT LOVELY?" THEO gushed, standing back and admiring the church altar they'd just covered with evergreen and holly.

"Yes!" Miss Alicia agreed, slipping her arm through Theo's. "How clever of you to think of gathering from the woods between the Hall and the church, so we didn't have to go anywhere near that fearful spot." She shivered at the thought.

"Very clever," Lord Whittington agreed from his perch on a ladder, wrapping greenery around an aisle column.

Miss Giles stood below Whittington, supplying greens as needed. "Is that where your sister is?" she asked, "Walking about looking for ghosts?"

Ignoring the censure in Miss Giles' words Theo defended, "She's investigating."

"The appearance of a toy?" Miss Giles laughed.

"There's more to it," Theo argued, "E sees things others miss."

"Well," Miss Giles huffed, "the next time I come across a discarded cuddly bear I will run to her for information."

"You may mock," Theo challenged, "but she's read every single science book in Father's library and remembers it all!"

Busy hanging greenery, adjusting ribbons and bows, no one appeared to be listening to the argument, other than quick sidelong glances. Until this moment. Hands stood motionless, bodies stilled. All but their faces, now turned toward Theo, mouths gaping, eyes wide.

The vicar recovered first, clearing his throat, "Every science book? Just how large is this library." He chuckled, "A few?" Everyone eased, chuckling among themselves, turning back to tasks at hand.

"The walls of Father's library are all books, some quite ancient, as well as more current..." The room stilled once more.

She'd done something wrong, but she wasn't quite certain what. Exuberance stalled, she changed tack, "It's not gone to waste, she started a parish school, to teach the tenant children."

"How..." Miss Alicia reached for words, "how, edifying," and nodded for the others to agree.

Lord Whittington was the one she worried about. She wanted him to hear of Eleanor's goodness, help him learn what she wasn't there to portray.

From his perch on the ladder, he asked, "Do you teach as well, Lady Theodora?"

Chin raised she proclaimed, "Yes. Yes, I do. But not the difficult subjects that Eleanor teaches. I teach the younger children how to read and do sums."

"My, you are a martyr!" Miss Giles said, handing Whittington some ribbon.

"Yes, I rather think they both are," he amended, "giving far beyond the expected."

"Waste of time, if you ask me," Lord Sudworth said, "what do the tenants need with such lessons?"

"To read the bible, perhaps?" the vicar chimed in, "Count change for their tithing?"

Whittington laughed. "How do you answer to that, Sudworth?"

"That's his job, to read the bible," Lord Sudworth responded good naturedly.

"And it is our job to decorate these blessed halls and tidy after ourselves," Theo said, gathering up the bits and pieces left from her efforts. "It is a shame Eleanor isn't here, she's a talented artist." Shooting a glance at Whittington, hoping he listened and agreed.

He was struggling with a bow Miss Giles handed him.

"My sister would have done something incredible with that bow," she tried again.

"A paragon," Miss Giles snapped.

"Would she?" Whittington's ignored the other woman.

"Oh, yes, her pictures are the exact image and she draws them so fast."

"Really?" the vicar asked, "quite clever of her to master both science and art."

"A gem of a young woman," Whittington added, smiling down on Theo, "with a delightful champion."

Theo blushed. He may have meant her, but from where she stood, he was the champion. Eleanor was the luckiest of women.

SIR FRANCIS HANDED Eleanor up into the carriage, before climbing in behind her. Bayford watched as Eleanor sat beside him, Sir Francis across from them.

"Anything?" the older man asked.

"Nothing," Eleanor adjusted the lap rug over her legs. "The sketch was as accurate as I could make it, but nobody recognized, or had seen, the boy."

Sir Francis studied the drawing, "This is the boy, you caught his likeness well."

"It hasn't helped. I'd so hoped it would."

Lady Eleanor had taken the forlorn bear to Greystone Manor that morning. Lady Grey recognized it immediately, reaching for it, tears pooling.

"This is not Briden's." Voice quivering, she traced the tiny bone buttons, "Briden's bear had moons," she lifted it, for Eleanor to see, "these buttons are stars."

"Russian?" Eleanor asked.

Surprised, Lady Grey looked up, "Yes. You could tell by the shirt? My mother's mother was Russian. My uncle made the bears as his uncle had made them for his children."

"I see," Lady Eleanor started to take the toy back, but Lady Grey pulled it to her chest, as Lord Grey entered the room.

"What is it, Anna," he'd asked.

"Thompson," she clung to the bear, "Thompson's bear. His buttons are stars."

"Is that his? Good God!" Lord Grey steadied himself with a chair back, "Good God!"

"What?" Lady Eleanor asked, but Sir Francis shook his head, stopping her from asking more. "What?" she whispered to him.

Sir Francis cleared his throat, "I take it Lord Thompson is your son?"

Their son, Lord Thompson, was nowhere to be found.

The toy had not been missing for two years. It was not Briden's.

It had been missing for a day. As long as their son had been gone.

"It's that Tom Baker's doing!" Lord Grey suddenly railed. "He's come back, I know he has. Who else would have done this?"

"Could the child have wandered off?" Sir Francis asked.

"We've looked everywhere. The child is gone!" Grey shouted.

"You think Tom Baker has returned?" Sir Francis asked.

"Who else would steal my son but him? He thinks I purposely drowned his son. Ridiculous. There was no evidence!" Lord Grey groused, "Doubt if he even had a son. Just wanted compensation, didn't he? Well, I sent him packing."

"After the drowning?" Eleanor's father tugged on his ear. Something he did when words didn't ring entirely true, "You said there was no drowning, nothing to fault, yet you believe this man seeks revenge?"

Lord Grey sniffed, twitched his nose, "Extortion didn't work, did it. Seeking ransom." He did not look at Bayford. He didn't look at anyone, other than quick piercing glances at his sorrowful wife. If she felt them, she took no notice. Tears slipped quietly down her cheeks, her eyes set on the bedraggled toy in her lap.

"Has he appealed for funds?" Francis asked.

"No," Lady Grey finally looked up, "and he never came after the flood. Nothing from Tom Baker. He could not have returned to the village without someone seeing him. No one has, not to this day."

"He went into the navy?" Sir Francis asked.

Lord Grey's gaze swung to Sir Francis, "Why do you ask that?"

"That's what we were told," Lady Eleanor said, "but no one on the staff at St. Martins knows him, or of him. Only a few of your people ever applied to them for work."

"Of course they wouldn't." Grey said, "Don't need servants when you're never there."

Lady Grey shook her head, before turning her attention back to the bear, "There have been no demands, no requests, nothing of the sort," she said, "We have no reason to believe Tom's responsible."

"He's here somewhere, I know it!" her husband barked.

"All I want is my son, safe and sound," she whispered, "I want my son returned safe, to be safe, with me, his mother." It was her turn to send a piercing glance at her husband. He flinched, a tick of his cheek, and turned to the window.

"That's why these people are here," Lord Grey explained, his back to the room. "We'll have him back right as rain. We will find him."

Eleanor sat with Lady Grey, "Tell me, about his disappearance."

"Probably just ran off and got himself lost." His father contradicted himself.

"Never!" Lady Grey glared, "He was four years old! His governess and nurse never let him out of their sight."

"Well they did now, didn't they?" he said.

Ignoring him, Lady Grey told Eleanor. "He was napping."

"And woke from that nap, perhaps explored, on his own," Sir Francis suggested.

Slowly Lady Grey shook her head, "Impossible. There are gates," she explained, "he'd have to go through the nursery and the latch on that door was out of his reach."

"The bastard got into the manor and stole him right..."

"Enough," Lord Bayford said, "we will assess how he was removed." Grey snorted.

"Just find him, please," Lady Grey pleaded once more, "just find him."

They scoured the nursery, spoke to the nursery maid, the nanny, his governess. No one knew how he could have gotten free of the room without help.

"Did you know Tom Baker?" she asked the servants but, as though rehearsed, each ducked their head, shaking it, backing away.

They knew Tom Baker. They knew more about Tom Baker than their job was worth.

Before they left, Lady Eleanor sketched his likeness from a portrait in the gallery. Grey's people had already taken it around Greystone Village, so they'd taken it to every village between Greystone and St. Martins Hall. They spoke to servants and tenants. None knew of Tom Baker or had seen a stranger recently.

None had seen the child.

But they'd heard one, when they walked from the village to old lady Scruggs place. They were standing in the woman's yard, speaking with her, when the peal of childish laughter washed over them followed by a hushing.

"He's dead," old lady Scruggs cocked her head toward the sound. "He's wit' the udder one."

One child's voice had become two, rising up as if from the ground. Giggling, shrieks of delight.

"There are no such thing as ghosts and ghouls," Lady Eleanor murmured, shivering away a chill lodged on her spine. "No such thing," yet, even as she said it, a child's shriek echoed through the woods.

Pivoting, she scanned the area, searching for the source.

"Won't fin' it, you won't," old lady Scruggs' son claimed, "We's all looked. Comes from nowhere."

"Oh, it comes from somewhere," Eleanor had murmured, hard pressed to spot the source.

They'd returned to the carriage then, as the church bell tolled.

"Sir Francis," she'd said, "last time we heard the child the clock had just tolled four."

"And it just tolled four again?" he handed her up into the carriage.

She settled beside her father who'd waited in the carriage.

"We've done as much as possible for today," he said, "we must hurry to return in time for tea."

"Wouldn't want to miss tea," Sir Francis murmured, across from them. "All that delightful company."

"No doubt," Eleanor challenged. Sir Francis had been exceptionally broody and cynical, if that were possible.

"I suppose we must," her father leaned back, "I can't help but wonder..."

"The cries?" Eleanor asked.

"You heard cries?" he asked. She nodded. "How interesting. But no, I hadn't realized. I was just thinking of that trip we took to Shropshire. When we hiked through the country."

"And those funny little places built into the rock," Eleanor remembered. "Those were odd. Did something now, make you think of those?"

Bayford patted her knee. "Hmmmm, what?" She'd lost him in thought. Doubted he was even listening to her. He was like that, so very different in his investigation. She followed facts, triggered by the smallest of items out of place. He jumped to conclusion without the least bit of logic. He was on target as often as she.

"Did you catch that sweet smell?" he asked, "What do you think the woman was baking?"

"Scruggs, do you mean?" Eleanor asked, "She wasn't baking at all. There was no smoke from her chimney."

"Wasn't there?" Sir Francis asked. "I hadn't looked but it's brittle out. Surely she'd have a fire against the chill."

"No smoke," Eleanor confirmed and sat back to wonder about it.

"We did catch her returning home," Sir Francis mused.

"Such a sweet smell," Bayford remembered, "same as the baker's room at the hall. Tasty treats, those were." He fell back to his own thoughts.

Eleanor sorted through her own. There had been something, that small little something, she just needed to shake it out of her memory. It refused to budge.

"I'm sorry you were pulled away from the festivities, El," her father said, "this was to be your Christmas, yet here you are..."

"In her element," Sir Francis reminded him.

"Not when it involves a child!" She took umbrage.

"No, of course not," he frowned, "no one wants the innocent harmed. That's not the point."

"Then what is?" she challenged him.

He smiled that knowing, superior smile, "You would have hated it if there'd been a tangle like this in another neighborhood and you hadn't been allowed to attend it."

He was right, but rather than acknowledge the fact, she looked out the window. The day had grown dim and, once more, she'd kept her father out and about when she should have sent him home hours ago. She promised him, "We'll be back at the manor soon. Warm fire, comfy seats."

"Yes, yes," he nodded and she realized the carriage movement was rocking him to sleep. Eleanor tucked his cover more securely around him. No use adjusting the foot warmers, they would be cold by now. She hadn't even tried to put hers in place.

"You wear him out," Francis said, not unkindly. She tossed a pillow he caught mid-air.

"He was not young when you were born." He reminded her. It wasn't a question. Anyone could see it. Her father had grown quite old in the past few years.

"He used to lead me about on investigations." She told him, wistful for days gone by. Nothing was quite so simple anymore.

"Now you lead him."

"He didn't even leave the carriage to query the people," she sighed. Her father used to enjoy watching people, learning about them.

"He trusts you."

It was more than that. It was getting too hard to navigate carriage steps. Her father wasn't so old as he was failing. She suspected his chess games with Mr. Fortnum, the physician, were about more than playing chess. Her father wasn't well.

"I trust you as well." Sir Francis offered.

Eleanor's eyes shot up. "Why wouldn't you?"

He chuckled. "In case you haven't noticed, you are a female. A gender prone to emotion over logic. Intellect and acumen are neither recognized, nor welcomed in the female."

"I should thank you?" she asked, eyebrows raised.

"More to the point, will your future husband both appreciate and encourage your budding talents?"

"Budding talents?" she yelped, lowering her voice when her father snuffled and shifted, "I wouldn't marry someone who didn't."

That infuriating eyebrow lift of his, as if to say, *"Is that so?"* when he knew the exact opposite.

He knew nothing.

"Lord Whittington may not understand my... interests," she explained, "but he is open to them."

"A rare man," Sir Francis dipped his head.

Smiling she asked, "You are giving me your blessing? Thank you."

"No," he leaned back against the squabs, lowered his tricorn to hide his eyes as if he were going to nap as well, "No, I was not giving you my blessing." And said no more.

Why had he said that? Whatever did he mean? Uncertainty stalled any temptation for a good set-down. She studied him instead. Theo had thought him excellent, when they met the robbers.

Was he too old for Theo? Good grief, of course he was. He was too old for Eleanor. Theo was not yet twenty; the man must be twice her age. All of forty at the least. Good god, he could be her father!

Chapter 4 ~ Courtship Woes

"What a wonderful reminder of the past," Theo exclaimed. "Ruins, here, of all places. What fun."

He wished they were at a ruin, but they weren't. They were in the center of St. Martins, his home. Its condition was the reason he and his father spent their time everywhere else.

He watched her, and his cousin Alicia, leaning over the balustrade, calling to Miss Giles below, waving their kerchiefs. Two young women, just starting out in life. They would both be snatched up quickly, once at court.

Which would be soon.

"Oh! I've dropped my token!" Alicia cried, pushing past him to the balcony stairs.

Laughing, he watched his cousin disappear when an ominous tremble, a smattering of rocks hitting the floor below, threw him into panic. Even as he turned to Lady Theodora her shriek filled the great hall. Pinwheeling backward, she fought sliding down a stone floor, flat moments ago, now sloping away.

"Theo!" he shouted, leaping forward, grabbing her around the waist, sweeping her into his hold.

He knew these walls, how they shifted and broke. A minor shower of stones little forewarning for a torrent of broad slabs slamming down, lethal.

"Out of the way!" he shouted to everyone, anyone who could hear him, as the balustrade gave way, the floor Theo had been standing on shuddering and breaking away, crashing below them.

Burrowing into his hold, Lady Theodora clung, turning her face just enough to peek at the gapping space. Dust billowed, a pungent cloud of ancient stone and debris.

"Was anyone hurt?" He shouted, choking on the air.

"Lady Theo!" Alicia, foolish girl, charged back up the stairs, "Are you hurt?" Joining them, enclosing Theodora in their hold.

"Alicia," he bit out, wanting to reprimand her for facing the danger of the stairs. Who knew if they'd hold any more than balcony had.

"No one hurt below," a breathless Alicia confirmed, "we all saw what was happening.".

"Good," he nodded, to shaken to move, "good." But he must move. He must lead these young ladies back down those steps, and away from any more danger. "These old stones are not at all secure," he explained, "trust I have you now, will lead you to safety."

Lady Theodora shuddered, fought for breath. He didn't fault her. She'd nearly toppled from the musician's gallery onto the great room floor. It would have killed her.

"You'll be fine now," he promised, impressed a young woman so full of enthusiasm did not fall prey to dramatic hysterics. In fact, not so much as a tear. She eased free of his hold, breathing with great deliberation, steadying herself before she looked up.

His world shifted. His heart stopped. He, too, found it hard to breathe, but for a very different reason. Who knew that the child following him around years ago would grow to take his breath away.

Then she looked away. "Forgive me, Lord Whittington."

Forgive her for what?

She avoided his eyes. Shy? Horrified by the dilapidated state of his home? Unable to face him? Pitying him?

She knew why he was marrying. Why he must marry her sister. The condition of his purse was no secret.

He wanted her to look at him again, as she had for that one moment. That fleeting moment of time, suspended in his heart. He'd felt like a knight of old, who'd rescued the damsel. He felt wondrous and strong and a true gallant.

With one glance.

There was no such look anymore. Just quick, guilty, glances.

"Please, forgive me, I was careless and have damaged your..." her eyes set on what was once a balustrade and floor. "Oh, my..."

"It is I who should apologize, Lady Theodora. This part of St. Martins is old. Too old for exploration and yet I brought you here," he confessed, "this was not your fault, but my error, allowing you into the gallery."

"Oh, no!" she argued, "It was splendid fun, and the adventure, of almost falling," she looked away again before squaring her shoulders and facing him. "Thank you, for catching me. I think I would have gone over the side without your help."

No more adoring looks. They were back to where they should be.

One leg back the other pointed before him he bowed low, "At your service, my fair damsel."

Theo and Alicia laughed, though Theo was gracious enough to say, "And my true knight. How brave you were." As he stood, she pulled a ribbon from her hair, "A token."

He took it, before she could change her mind, tucking it between the buttons of his vest. Their return to friendship. He the brother-in-law to be.

For he'd be marrying her sister. He was not sorry for it. Lady Eleanor would make a fine duchess. If she proved as engaging as her younger sister, they would fare well. If her passion for life equaled Theodora's, and if that passion translated into other areas of life, the marriage would be more than acceptable.

But it was wrong of him to compare. Lady Eleanor was grown. Theo barely beyond childhood. He smiled at her, as a doting brother would.

The soft mounds of her bosom, rising from her bodice, trembled with the fear that had not quite left. The ripe bosom of a woman. He shifted his gaze.

Eleanor had the height, the stature of a duchess. Theo was delicate and innocent and childlike. He would take Theo and his cousin under his wing. After all, one was family and the other would become family and....

Eleanor was there, in the flesh, sweeping through the doorway into the room. Stately and composed. Wonderful. A veritable duchess. A flesh and blood target for his interest. He needed her about him, he needed her there, a real woman, a reality, and here she was.

"Look, my ladies," he told Theo and Alicia, "Lady Eleanor has offered her presence." He bowed to her, "Have you found your answers?"

But she hadn't. Her pensive gaze an ominous warning.

"He's teasing, E," Theo prompted.

"Are you?" Lady Eleanor asked, blinking, relaxing into a smile, "I'm afraid the humor's been drained from me this morning. Rather a dreadful situation."

"Absolutely," Whittington mirrored her seriousness, "of course. Something has developed?"

"You found the bear's mother?" Miss Giles asked, with false wide eyes.

"In a manner of speaking," Lady Eleanor explained. "We were visiting Lord and Lady Grey. Apparently, the bear belongs to her son, Lord Thompson, who is missing. Has been, this past day."

"Oh, E!" Theo gasped.

"Yes, it is a worry," Eleanor admitted.

Whittington made his way to where Lady Eleanor waited. She must think him abominable. Leaving her and her father to trouble over these matters while he pursued frivolity. His behavior totally inappropriate. But someone had to host the group and keep their spirits on the festive season.

He joined her, with just that argument, "I've been distracted by the season. Forgive me for not taking your concerns with the proper seriousness," he offered, feeling rather like a child, caught out by the adults.

"Of course," Eleanor beamed now, rather taking his breath away. Her smile washed away years. "It was just a toy. Who would have thought it relevant? And you've all been decorating the hall. We've just passed through, everything so festive and lovely and here I come, bringing in the drearies. Forgive me please!"

"No, no!" Miss Giles exclaimed, "we expect that of you. Lady Theodora claims you are an expert. That your papa relies on you."

Lady Eleanor looked down her nose, just as a duchess should. Whittington bit back a laugh.

"I assist my father, that is all. Unfortunately, we were unable to conclude our findings."

"Not at all?" Whittington asked. "The boy's still not found?"

"No, not as yet."

"We will send men to the Grey's, to help with the search. For now, let us instill a touch of the season. You've missed too much of it." He led her and the others out of the old keep.

No one, not the ones touring the ruined hall, nor Lady Eleanor who'd arrived to a light cloud of dust, mentioned the crash of the balcony. Despite Lady Eleanor's propensity for investigating the unusual, searching for meaning in a misplaced toy, she refrained from questioning a near disaster. Not a query to be heard.

He should be relieved at everyone's restraint. All far too polite to embarrass the future Duke of Summerton, with his crumbling walls. They'd not speak of it in his presence, not until his back was turned.

Time to end tours to this part of the castle. The other wings would have to suffice. Except he didn't quite know how those other wings fared.

"We must rehearse for the play," he distracted them all.

"Play?" Eleanor blinked.

"Oh, yes, El," Theo cried, "it will be great fun! The girls will dress as boys and the boys as women and…"

"I see," Eleanor looked a bit stunned, "and we play these parts?" She asked Whittington.

"You don't have to," he offered, "there are roles besides those on stage."

"More comfortable, perhaps, for me," her smile didn't ring true.

"It will be fun," he promised, though he was beginning to think it wouldn't. Not quite. Not for Eleanor. She was the audience sort. A rather stern audience sort. An adult watching the children play.

"The youngsters need supervision," he hedged, "and I thought we would help."

"The youngsters?" she frowned, "From the nursery?"

"Yes," he failed to pique her interest. "You do like children, don't you?" he asked.

"Of course I do," she said, though he wasn't certain he believed her, "in the nursery. They will have their governesses and tutors?"

"Of course." He looked to Theo.

"Eleanor is very good with children," she defended, "she raised me, didn't you E?"

"You were a delight!" Eleanor laughed, "But I've no experience with raucous boys."

"No, of course you wouldn't," Whittington agreed, relieved, "you will have help. Let's go below stairs, to the music room."

HE FOUND THEM IN THE music room, creating chaos, Lady Eleanor in the midst of it, brow furrowed, watching Lady Theo, Miss Alicia and Lord Sudworth making fools of themselves… acting, that was it, they must be acting. Sir Francis decided not to interrupt. Far too amusing to see Eleanor as… whoever she was meant to be.

"Sir Francis." Whittington spotted him, spoiling his fun.

But there were other priorities. "Lady Eleanor's father is looking for her," he bowed.

"Unfortunately, we've confiscated her, she's to help with our performance," Whittington said, as if a performance held highest priority.

"If father wants me..." No doubt Eleanor wanted rescuing.

Sweet, spoiled, Theo butted in, "Don't let her go, Lord Whittington, or we'll never get her back."

And for good reason. "A performance?" Sir Francis asked, as if he hadn't figured it out, "As in a play, perhaps?"

"A farce, with music!" Miss Alicia clapped, "It will be such fun! We're all trading places so women will play men and men women and..."

"Enough, Miss Alicia," Whittington patted her head, "you will spill the tale before we've even begun. And I fear you've frightened Lady Eleanor."

"No," Eleanor shook her head, "of... of course not."

"See," Whittington laughed, "terrified!"

"You already said, Lady Eleanor doesn't have to perform. She will watch over the children. They'll be here soon." Miss Alicia explained, "No need to fear."

He'd be terrified. Care of brats? Eleanor burst out laughing, pointing at him, "Look! You've terrified Sir Francis with the mere talk of children!"

He did not rise to Eleanor's bait, "There is a child who needs her attention."

Whittington sobered, "You've found..."

Eye brow raised, Sir Francis shook his head.

"Really, sir," Whittington argued, "Allow her a chance to smile, to make merry. You and Lord Bayford ask too much of her. Surely the two of you can sort things out without her."

"I am merely her father's messenger," Sir Francis countered.

"Papa is like that, Lord Whittington, he does so depend on E," Theo explained, "but it's not fair, Sir Francis. Eleanor should be allowed a bit of fun."

"I am here," Eleanor pointed out, obviously annoyed of the conversation going on about her.

"Yes, you are," Whittington bowed, "and I'll not let them steal you away. Good grief, they had you out in the cold half the night!"

"I don't mind," she tried to tell him when he interrupted, "Go with your sister and the others. I will offer assistance in your stead."

"But..."

"No, off you go. Enjoy yourself!" he ordered.

Theo and Alicia crowed their delight, and grabbed Eleanor's hands, steering her away from the gentlemen.

Francis flexed his hands, tempted to physically pull her away when she looked over her shoulder at him, not Whittington, as if he could save her from the horrors of creating a farce.

"Shall we go?" Wittington's smiling voice so obtuse to the drama he created, Sir Francis had to look twice. "She will make a fine duchess."

The man was overconfident.

"You've made an offer for her hand?" Francis asked, knowing he hadn't.

"We are working on the details. Perhaps Christmas day." Whittington admitted, "But she knows, we both know, that is the course we will take."

"Why Lady Eleanor, surely there are grander prizes out there?" Sir Francis prodded, curious if the man saw both the challenge and wonder of the woman.

"She personifies what is needed in the House of Summerton; reserve, intelligence, others before self," Whittington reeled off his list, "this is Christmas, time for festivities, yet she had to be coerced to join in the fun of it. I'll not allow that! Fated to be a duke, I understand the weight of expectations. I need a wife who will face the task. In return, I will see that she not be crushed by those demands."

Idiot! Eleanor didn't give a fig for frivolity or idleness. She would be a damned fine duchess precisely because of that. She would welcome the weight of the station.

Sir Francis warned, "Unlike a moldable debutante, she will not divest of herself easily."

"I offer her joie de vivre! She needs but a taste!" he proclaimed.

"What of her father? Is she to abandon him?" Francis asked.

"Of course not! Lord Bayford needs assistance, I will assist." He put out his hand, directing Francis to precede him through a doorway. "She raised her sister, helps her father? When is she allowed moments for herself?"

"She attends the theater, has been known to enjoy country dances," Sir Francis offered.

"I should hope she enjoys more than that."

"She enjoys helping her father."

Whittington harrumphed, "Women must be allowed to be women. Pursue art and poetry and the delights of fashion. Even her gowns are pragmatic, so little lace or embroidery."

He didn't laugh, though it was a hard-fought resistance. Whittington wore enough lace and gold embroidery for two. He'd have to cover it up, as they were going a distance outside. Already in heavy traveling cape, tricorn and gloves, Sir Francis suggested, "You will need your outer coat, a warm one."

"Of course," Whittington snapped.

Sir Francis rolled his eyes and waited, as the Earl donned his outer wear, before leading him through the grounds, determined not to listen to his inane conversation anymore.

"Do you get to London much?" the Earl asked.

"No."

After a short silence, Whittington wondered, "Your waistcoat, did you get it on the continent?"

"A local seamstress."

"Ah," Whittington nodded, as if it made sense, "Do you care for whist?"

"No."

Finally, with a touch of irony, the young man suggested, "More used to your own company than society's. No wonder you expect Lady Eleanor to be like minded. You assume it is normal. I would argue, women are not so single minded."

That made him laugh. "You've no idea," Sir Francis told him, "none at all."

They reached Lord Bayford at the very spot the bear had been found. Whittington nonplussed, "You kept Lady Eleanor out here for hours, didn't even make it to supper, surely you've learned all you could from this place."

"As I said, you've not a clue," Sir Francis chuckled.

Confused, Bayford looked to Francis for help, but he wasn't about to help Whittington.

"What?" Whittington argued, "Is it so odd that I would doubt the wisdom of forcing a gently bred woman to stand in the cold as you searched for whatever you searched for?"

"Gently bred woman?" Lord Bayford asked.

"Yes," the younger Earl snapped, "your daughter!"

"Eleanor?" Bayford's dumbfounded question had Sir Francis laughing again. He was beginning to enjoy this little outing.

"That's enough," Whittington cut them both, "you may be a commoner," he condescended to Francis, "but you," he pointed to Bayford, "are an earl, and part of the Bayford family. I cannot believe Lady Eleanor has been raised as a work maid."

"Oh, no, no, no," her father shook his head, "absolutely not."

"You're causing embarrassment," Francis said.

"Embarrass who?" Whittington snapped, "Not Lady Eleanor, most certainly. She's the victim here. No one to champion her. That's about to change!"

"It's very difficult to raise daughters without their mother," Lord Bayford mourned, "Perhaps she could have stopped Eleanor..."

"Lady Eleanor is a force unto herself," Francis interjected, ignoring Whittington.

"Yes, yes, but a mother might have forbidden her where I did not," the older man moaned.

"Forbid her what?" Whittington asked.

Eyes rheumy with age, Lord Bayford looked up, "Her fascination with the physical sciences." He pulled a kerchief from his wrist, wiped his eyes, "She is so astute, so genuinely enthralled, I couldn't."

"You wouldn't have anyway," Francis reminded him, "you enjoyed her help."

Bayford chuckled, "Aye, I did. Do."

Whittington put his foot down with a resounding stomp, "My apologies, Lord Bayford, but I will not have you pulling her from the entertainments. She deserves to enjoy herself."

"Yes, she does," Bayford frowned, "This was to be her Christmas, her time for mirth and merriment. The trouble is, this," he pointed at the ground, "is her enjoyment."

Whittington looked down at the path to the lake. Frozen footprints, undergrowth trodden down by resting boats, sparkling with frost.

Good God, did the man really believe Eleanor preferred to stand here? No stories to tell, no comfort or joy of others, just a lonely, bitterly cold spot. "She enjoys pleasing you, Lord Bayford. It's time you set her free."

"You think she does this for me?" Bayford asked.

Brow up, eyes wide, astonished the question had to be asked, Whittington looked like a gaping fish.

"You don't understand Lady Eleanor," Francis argued, but Bayford put out his hand, to stay the man.

"Perhaps he understands her better than we," the older Earl said, "perhaps we've known her too long and refuse to see what is right before us."

"Don't be ridiculous!" Francis countered.

"You think I'm being ridiculous?" Whittington asked, "to think a woman might want to be entertained? Donning stylish attire instead of practical, plain ensembles? Have friendships?"

"She has friends!" Francis barked.

"Does she?" Bayford asked. "Name one."

"Well... the rector and his wife? And the teacher in the village, as well as..."

"Those are neighbors."

"The chit who married the Duke of Devonshire." Francis reminded.

Bayford considered, and smiled, "Yes, yes, they are quite fond of one another but, truth told, the friendship came via Theo. Theo and Georgianna are of an age."

"One friend?" Whittington exclaimed, "you had to search your minds to find one friend? She should have dozens. You should be counting them off with all fingers and toes."

"We don't read her correspondence." Francis defended.

"Then name Lady Theodora's friends," Whittington asked.

Bayford laughed, "As I said, The Duchess of Devonshire, Lady Jane, little Mary, Muffy and Rosalind and..."

"Do you see?" Whittington railed.

Rubbing his nose, Bayford relented, "I see. Yes, yes, hmmm. Her studies have kept her from the joys of fraternity."

"Studies? She takes care of you, of her sister and helps Sir Francis here with his investigations," Whittington had worked himself up to full throttle, "It's time you," he pointed at the magistrate, "solve your own crimes!" And stormed off, as though threatened by his own erupting anger.

His, not Lady Eleanor's.

Fool to fight the battles of a woman perfectly capable of fending for herself. Whittington wasn't defending his future wife, he was defending expectations. Preconceptions never lead to a good ending.

Sir Francis looked to his mentor, Lord Bayford. The old man knew it, but he fought that knowing.

Sorrier state of affairs, he'd yet to see.

Lady Eleanor was doomed.

Chapter 5 ~ Christmas Cheer, or Else

Every time Eleanor tried to get near her father or Sir Francis, Whittington would pull her over to meet another of his relatives. Or he would stop her to discuss a piece of art in the long gallery. Or confide a touch of gossip about some of his London friends.

If he wasn't tugging her one way or another, his cousin would, or Theo.

"You are allowed to have fun," Theo claimed.

Fun was relevant to the bearer.

Standing near the pianoforte watching carolers, primed to join them with "*and heaven and nature sing!*" Eleanor startled when her father touched her arm.

"Papa?"

"Come," he told her, shaking his head at Lord Whittington who spotted the interaction, primed to interrupt, as he'd done all evening. But he stayed back, this time.

The two walked the length of the gallery, Eleanor on her father's arm, mirrors reflecting the glittering light of chandeliers and branches of candles. They found a quiet corner, where her father could hear without competing with the swirl of other conversations.

"Enjoying yourself?" he asked.

And she was, in her own way. "Look at all the evergreen and ribbons." She twisted and turned to take it all in, "Theo helped with all this, and the scent," she drew in a long sniff, cinnamon and cloves, mingling with bees wax and brazier smoke. "Such a festive Christmas," she turned back, taking his hands, "but..." she wanted to speak of more serious business. He stopped her.

"Don't fret, little one, Sir Francis and I have everything in hand." He always called her little one though she was nearly half a head taller. "This Christmas is for you to enjoy."

"A child is missing," she pressed.

"Trust me, on this," he tapped his nose, "Tell me about the young Earl," he distracted, "what do you think of him, eh?"

"I like him," She did. Who wouldn't? He was all Theo said he was, handsome, kind, thoughtful and witty. "He and the Duke are marvels, so many entertainments." They were in the long gallery. A space filled with diversions. Carolers at the pianoforte, tables for whist, spillikins, fox and geese. Small, sitting areas, such as the one they occupied, for conversation.

"A shame the Duke is indisposed. I've visited him. Not comfortable, not one bit. But look at those two," Bayford gestured toward Theo and Alicia, "thoroughly enjoying themselves."

"A delight to witness," Eleanor agreed, as proud as any mama.

"Should I be delighted for you?"

"Oh, Papa," she squeezed his arm, "Of course," she exaggerated, for he seemed to need the assurance. She didn't explain the guilt, for standing comfortably amid such splendor while a child was out there somewhere, lost? In trouble? Held prisoner?

"With the Earl?"

Eleanor blinked. She'd forgotten about the Earl. "Yes, yes of course," she spotted him now, watching others at the cards table.

"He seems fond of you," her father said, "quite protective of your time."

She should be flattered, "I'm not familiar with such attentions."

"You should be," Bayford said, "I should have remarried and..."

"I'm rather glad you didn't. Is that terribly shellfish of me?" Eleanor asked.

He looked up, "No, my dear, not at all. I'm flattered. But don't you think you'd have liked a woman's touch in your life?"

"Pshaw," she brushed that aside. "We've been perfectly happy."

"Now you'll have a household of your own, eh?"

"The entertainments will be exhausting," she laughed, "but when people leave..."

"You'll have time for your investigations."

"What's this?" Sir Francis stepped into their conversation, "investigations? I thought we weren't to talk of such things with Lady Eleanor."

She hit his arm with her fan, "Don't be foolish, who would I be without my investigations?"

Her father looked at Sir Francis, who looked back at her. Neither responded. Before she could ask them just what that look meant Grimms stepped into the room, looking about, making a beeline for them.

"Oh, dear," Eleanor put her fan to her mouth, "oh dear."

Whittington abandoned the card table, reaching the butler before he reached them, signaling for Sir Francis to follow as he and the butler left the room.

"Papa?" Eleanor asked.

Her father rose, "I'll see what they're about."

"I'll join you."

"No," he patted her hand on his arm, "you stay here. We'll not be long."

Wasn't that what she always said to Theo, and then she'd take an age? She hesitated as Theo and Alicia flanked her.

"What do you think has happened," Theo asked, "do you think they've found the boy."

"I so hope so!" Alicia exclaimed, "I do hope so."

If wishes were horses, beggars would ride, the old saying rang in Eleanor's mind.

No, she didn't think they'd found the boy, but something important had happened.

HANDS OUT TO HER SIDES, Eleanor waited as her maid snipped the stitches attaching her stomacher to her dress. Theo, already in her nightrail and wrap, watched from the bench at the foot of the large canopied bed.

"Would you mind terribly if I were to sleep in Alicia's room?" she asked.

"Isn't Lady Alicia sharing with her mother?" Eleanor wondered.

"Her mother is in an adjoining room," Theo explained. "Now that she's a woman, she asked not to share a bed with her."

Even dressed to sleep, Theo sat straight, hands delicately folded in her lap, a poised young woman. How had it happened? There she was, days away from turning sixteen. Some of her friends already married. She wasn't asking to over-night with a friend to play with paper dolls. They would be whispering about handsome gentlemen, dreams of court and all sorts of imaginings carried from girlhood, waiting for a night such as this.

Gracie finished undressing her.

"Of course, you may change chambers for the evening," she offered magnanimously, aware of her loss. Theo, more daughter than sister, would soon have her own household. They'd live miles apart.

"You'll not be lonesome, without me?" Theo scowled, "And don't look so surprised. I know you. You'll be up all night trying to figure things out. If I were here I would send for something warm to drink or see that you've slippers and wrap."

"I am quite capable of caring for myself," Lady Eleanor reminded Theo, as she slipped her arms into the wrap Gracie held ready.

"You can take care of others well enough, you dismiss yourself. And you'll be fretting over what they found this evening."

Frustratingly true. "I don't know what that is, do I?"

"You always know, it's me they don't tell. Horrible thing not knowing," Theo fiddled with the silk ribbon at her neck. "Worse when you're alone." Her doldrums ended in a flash. Theo jumped up, "We will worry together! I'll invite Miss Alicia to stay here."

"No!" There had already been too many people today. Eleanor rubbed her neck, waiting as Gracie urged her to sit at the dressing table, where she pulled the heavy wig from her head.

Heaven.

"I'm sorry, Theo, I didn't mean to sound so harsh, but you are right. I will be thinking and I can't do that if the two of you are here."

Gracie pulled the skull cap off, freeing Eleanor's hair to fall, a mane of chestnut tendrils free from their tight confines, massaging her head.

Bliss.

"Thank you, Gracie, you may go now. I shan't need you again this evening."

Gracie bobbed and hurried out so quickly Eleanor wondered if there wasn't someone waiting.

"Whoever did this, is spoiling our Christmas," Theo cried.

Eyebrows raised, Eleanor caught her sister's eyes in the mirror, "Oh, of course," she lamented, "The Earl of Grey's household should keep their sorrows to themselves. Our 'fun' is of the utmost importance."

Theo looked away, but only for a moment before she persisted, "I don't mean my fun. Honestly, I didn't. This was to be your Christmas with Lord Whittington. You could lose him, because of this ghastly business. You are not attending to him as you must!"

"No?" Eleanor asked, "Am I not attending to him by helping to alleviate shadows? Do I not prove my worth just as well by that as by dressing up as a young man and dancing about in a play?"

They stared at each other, neither right or wrong.

"You must marry him." Theo's voice was small, buried in unshed tears.

"Oh, sweet one," Eleanor abandoned the dressing table, hurrying to her sister, "What sort of marriage would I have if I could not do my studies?"

"At least you would have a marriage," Theo said.

Theo's harsh reality stung. Two and twenty was a ripe age for a maiden. More like a spinster. But she wasn't lonely. She had purpose.

Theo snapped, completely out of character. "Your first real suitor and he is perfect! Absolutely perfect!"

"Perhaps I'm not perfect enough for him." She'd accepted the marriage would happen. What if Theo had the right of it, that she risked the union?

"You are just as perfect as he is," Theo defended.

"Am I?" Eleanor rocked back on her heels. "I'm beginning to wonder."

She had to marry, for Theo. To offer consequence and the protection of her name. Her father and aunt would fail terribly as sponsors. Theo was superb, the finest England had to offer. She deserved the highest level of society. Eleanor's marriage was her only hope of reaching it.

Theo rose, pulling Eleanor upright. Of the two of them, Theo had the tears, swiping at them even as they dried on her cheeks, "I know what we need to do. I will not abandon you tonight. I will stay here until we come up with a plan, to show your attributes, how perfect you are."

Good lord, was she so inept? "Please, don't. I will think on it. You know how I am when thinking. The candles burn all night. You'd get no sleep."

"You need to sleep. You barely managed to last night."

"Go!" Eleanor insisted.

Theo's chin quivered as she stood firm.

"I promise you, I will think on it," Eleanor pressed, pushing at her sister, "go."

"Maybe Alicia can..."

"No, do not discuss this with her. She is his cousin. I will come up with a plan."

"Are you certain?" Theo asked.

"Yes, now go!" Eleanor ordered.

With a fierce hug, Theo said good night and left, knowing better than argue once Eleanor made up her mind.

Alone, Eleanor opened the window, leaning over the ledge, drawing in clear, bracing air. So cold it hurt her lungs, but she didn't care. Stars, pure and bright, stood out against the black sky of a new moon.

There was goodness in the world. She was certain of it. Look at Lord Whittington, sweet in his attempts to teach her how to have fun when she was such a poor student. It all seemed so silly, play acting. Excitement over a hand at cards, as if a whimsical draw of a heart or spade merited joy or sorrow. Irrelevant, when a child was missing.

She closed the window, leaned her forehead to the cold pane, wanting so much for Theo. Shamed, for even that couldn't stop her curiosity, her hunger to find reason and solutions.

Reaching under her sleeping cap, she rubbed her scalp, aching from bearing the weight of her hair either tugged to the sky, or squashed in a tight cap.

Someone knocked on her door. Not the scratch of a servant. A true knock. Firmer than her father's. Certainly not Theo, who'd push through, no polite warning.

Lord Whittington perhaps?

Foolish thought. He wouldn't risk such a thing before declaring himself.

One longing glance at the handle of the bed warmer protruding from the promise of the turned down bed, Eleanor pulled her wrap firmly closed and adjusted her sleeping cap.

Impossible to discount Lord Whittington entirely. Perhaps something 'fun' occurred to him. Another venture he wished to educate her to.

She opened the door and peeked out.

"Your father wondered if you would join him in the study," Sir Francis asked.

She opened the door wider, "Let me get my slippers." He waited by the open door as she slipped on mules she'd just taken off. "Please tell me everyone else has gone to bed and I shan't need to don more than this night wrap."

"We'll take the servants' stairs," he offered.

With a roll of her eyes, she looked over her shoulder, eyebrows raised, ready to tell him that wasn't an answer, but he was watching her with such intensity, curiosity shooed words away.

"What?" she asked.

Gentleman enough not to glance up and down her formless nightwear, he was not so good to refrain from stepping forward, turning her to face him and flicking her night cap, "Hiding all that hair under there?"

"Yes!" She grabbed hold of the cap, pushing it firmly back in place. It hadn't been easy to get all of her hair under the protective muslin. It was one of Theo's. Her own cap had been left behind, tucked by habit under her pillow at home. Out of sight, the maid failed to pack it. Eleanor readjusted everything again, felt for the ribbon that kept it tied about her head.

"Lady Eleanor?" Whittington popped his head in the door, gaze going from Francis to Eleanor, "is anything amiss?'

Nothing but my attire. "No," Eleanor shot a warning glance at Sir Francis, "my father asked if I could join him for a... a..."

Chuckling, Sir Francis helped her, "He likes to have a small brandy before bed. Eleanor usually joins him."

Good lord, what was Sir Francis implying, "I do not imbibe regularly..."

This time, Lord Whittington finished for her, chuckling himself, "A wee dram encourages Morpheus, does it not, Sir Francis?"

"It does indeed," the older man agreed.

"If you two will excuse me," she shooed them out.

"We will wait outside," Lord Whittington bowed, "while you change."

Eleanor blinked. She'd sent Gracie to bed and Theo wasn't there. How was she going to change on her own?

"Please, do not wait, I will be there shortly," she shut the door.

Sir Francis stopped it from closing, "We will wait."

"How gallant, but I must insist, do go ahead of me." She pushed hard, shut the door, sorry she didn't hear a yelp. It would have served him right if she'd caught his fingers.

And why did Whittington speak for her, finishing her sentences, as if she weren't even there?

It took nearly an hour to dress with help. Impossible without it. Slips and hoops she could manage but how was she to put all the pieces together, fasten bodice to stomacher, by herself?

Bother, drat and bother! She swung around, searching for a solution and there it was, draped over the back of a chair. The Summerton household was frugal with fires and, even if lit for her father, it took an age to burn off the chill of a large room. No one would look amiss if she wore her cape into the room. Gracie had cleaned the heavy velvet and fur to perfection and it was easy to don.

Hair was another concern. She yanked the night-cap's bow, unfastening the ribbon and pulled the thing from her head. Her hair flopped down her back, waves flattened from being under the skull cap earlier. She bent forward, rustled it and flipped back. Almost, but she didn't want it pulled back. With another thorough fluffing she readjusted it to cascade over one shoulder.

Much better than the misshapen bulges and knobs under the cap. She would do.

Finding her out-of-doors cap, she perched it on her head, settled her cape on her shoulders, fastened the ties to keep it closed and hurried off to meet the gentlemen.

"LOOK!" ALICIA CRIED, "a falling star!"

"Oh, wish!" Theo cried, "Wish for my sister and your cousin."

Alicia frowned, "I think it's too late. You're supposed to wish when you see it, before it fades."

Theo considered and had to agree. Not that wishing on stars would help. Eleanor taught her that prayers and wishes were all very good, but one had to put actions to desires.

"We'll think of something," Alicia consoled.

They'd spent the evening discussing Eleanor and Whittington. "She's too responsible not to solve a problem," Theo mourned.

"That's a good thing, isn't it?" Alicia asked, "Whittington would know that. Being responsible is a perfect trait for a duchess. And Mama says he needs to marry her."

That only made Theo feel worse. She needed him to *want* to marry Eleanor. It had to be perfect, but it wouldn't be perfect if E wasn't there to fall in love with.

All Eleanor had to do was act like a normal lady. Push her exceptional self aside for a time. Be lovely and sweet with all her attention on Whittington. Men liked to be thought of, considered. To be the most important thing in a woman's world.

Someone else had to find out where that missing boy was. Anyone but Eleanor.

"What's that?" Alicia asked, pointing out toward the woods that led to Briden's Lake.

"What?" Theo strained to see in the darkness. "Where?"

"The lantern, on the path," Alicia pointed.

There it was, the bob of a lantern visible through the winter barren trees.

"Oh, no!" Theo cried.

"What?" Alicia asked.

"We tried so hard to keep her from the investigation tonight that she's gone off on her own, now."

"Never!" Alicia gasped, "Not into the haunted woods, by herself!"

Theo nodded mournfully, "That's precisely what she would do. And I know a secret no one else knows."

"A secret?" Alicia whispered.

Theo nodded slowly, "Eleanor hates woods at night. She'd never go by herself, not without someone to protect her."

Both girls looked out the window. A lone lantern was disappearing down the slope.

"Maybe it's not her," Alicia offered.

"Maybe," Theo doubted it, "but there's one way to find out." She left the window seat and headed for the door.

"Where are you going?" Alicia hissed.

"To my chamber, to see if Eleanor is there," Theo explained.

"And if she's not?"

"I'll do nothing," Theo told her, "unless her cape is gone. If that's gone, then so is she. I'll go and find her. She'll need me."

Alicia cringed back in the window seat, "You can't, you mustn't, you..."

"Don't worry," Theo soothed, "as you said, it's probably not Eleanor."

"Of course it isn't," Alicia relaxed, "you said she hates to go into woods alone. She would have taken someone with her."

"Yes," Theo said, "she would have. I'll just go and see if she's in our chamber and, if not, assure myself her cape is there."

"I'll come with you," Alicia bravely promised.

Eleanor wasn't in her chamber, nor was her cape or cap. She had left, to go outside, all alone.

ELEANOR STEPPED INTO the study, frowning at her father's raspy snore. Sir Francis, standing at the wall of books, saluted her with his drink, a volume of some sort in his other hand, "Welcome," he said. Whittington had been studying the fire but looked up and smiled, holding up his drink, "A tipple for you?"

An empty glass sat on the table beside her father who was slumped, chin on chest, in a chair near Whittington. His shallow breath rattled, shaming her for keeping him out too long the night before.

Lifting a lap robe from the back of another chair, she tucked it about her father.

"Is that you, Eleanor?" He opened his eyes, patted her hand. "You took your time."

"I was ready for bed," she explained.

"Of course, you would be," he nodded. "but I thought you'd want to know what we learned."

"Yes," she told him, "I would, but Sir Francis can tell me."

"Let's not trouble Lady Eleanor with this business," Lord Whittington abandoned the fire for the drinks tray.

A large, billowing fire, high and full and warm. So very warm. Too warm for a fur cape.

"Does that trouble you?" Sir Francis asked Whittington.

"It does trouble me," Whittington admitted, pouring two brandies.

"I want to hear," she admitted.

His smile did not reach his eyes as he handed Eleanor a tumbler.

"Bayford," Whittington continued, "free her of this business, of always caring for others. A lady must have time for herself."

Fingers on the spine of a book, about to pull it from the shelf, Sir Francis cocked his head and turned, skewering Whittington with such scorn Eleanor shifted, took the seat across from her father, her back to Sir Francis.

She felt his approach, her neck prickling when he stopped behind her chair, heat rising in her cheeks when he placed his hands on the back of it. Sir Francis was subtle. The slightest of movements conveyed a world of meaning she would miss by sitting as she had.

"She does, doesn't she?" he drawled, so out of the blue Eleanor had to think back to Whittington's inaccurate portrayal of her. It was nonsense. Her problem was an obsessive curiosity, that had her forgetting the care of those she loved, not martyrdom.

"I am here, you know," she reminded them all.

"Yes," Sir Francis drawled, "I'm well aware of that."

Drat! She twisted around to see why Lord Whittington flushed, his jaw flexed, but Frances was his droll self.

"I do what?" she challenged Francis.

"Saturate yourself in troublesome cases."

"Exactly!" Whittington proclaimed.

"But that's not to please her father," the magistrate explained, "I've known him to look for a snarl of offenses, somewhere, anywhere, just to keep her happy."

"He does not!" she objected.

"He does," Sir Francis was enjoying this conversation a bit too much.

"There's no time for such things if one is a wife and mother, let alone a duchess." Lord Whittington explained.

Eleanor learned, for the first time, how words can be frozen in the throat. She couldn't quite breathe.

"Which is why she'd be better off married to me." Sir Francis dropped his comment with the ease of flicking lint, stopping her breath entirely. In fact, it sucked the air out of the entire room. Even her father sat up, leaning forward, as if to soundlessly say, "Come again?"

Which is why she'd be better off married to me ...

Wherever had he gotten that idea? He was her father's friend, albeit younger but not that young. They bickered, constantly.

And investigated crimes.

She mustn't forget the reason for his... what? A proposal? Was it a statement of intent?

She blinked, as the others started to rally.

"See here," Lord Whittington coughed away a chuckle, not taking Sir Francis seriously.

You always took Sir Francis seriously. Even his humor was serious. No words wasted on frivolity.

On the other hand, he may have been poking Lord Whittington to action. Rushing things, forcing him to confront the issue at hand; Eleanor's investigations. They made her what she was, an investigator.

Her father coughed as well, but he wasn't hiding humor. In fact, his was fighting horrific congestion. The effort mottling his cheeks. On her knees, beside him, Eleanor rubbed his back as he leaned forward, choking into his kerchief.

"There, there, Papa," she soothed, scowling at Sir Francis for riling him.

"I only spoke the truth," he countered.

"We shall see," Lord Whittington challenged. Theo would have been pleased by the force of his conviction.

No, no, not Theo, *she* was pleased. Of course, she was, it proved dedication. No matter how obtuse, his motives were pure. He was championing her, in his way.

More gently, Whittington asked Eleanor, "Should I send for the housekeeper? A tonic for your father?"

"Give him your brandy." Sir Francis handed her the glass she'd left behind, his idea of a tonic, "this will calm him."

Much as she'd prefer the ground swallowing Francis whole, a tipple was her father's medicinal choice. "Thank you," she grudgingly took it.

Her father waved it away, pressing his kerchief to his mouth for one last shuddering cough before leaning back. Free of the violent spasms he now flicked his hand, beckoning brandy. Eleanor pressed it into his trembling hold, helping him lift it to his mouth.

Worst over, Eleanor told Whittington, "You needn't bother the housekeeper. I'm certain he's better now."

"If you're..."

Eleanor's father waylaid whatever Lord Whittington meant to say, "Back to your bed, Eleanor," he harrumphed, "Whittington will you see my daughter to her door?"

Sir Francis straightened, ready to join them.

"Not you Sir Francis. We need to have a word."

Predictable as ever, his eyebrow raised in amused condescension, Sir Francis returned to his negligent lean by the bookcase. Lord Whittington looked at him as if he were an offensive coiled snake. Not necessarily a viper but certainly unwanted.

Her father would put Sir Francis in his place. Perfectly fine with her, except she wished to speak with her father about what had happened that evening. What had Grimms wanted? The servants weren't talking. She daren't ask Lord Whittington, though he would know.

Oh, drat! He really would be a troublesome husband, turning everything inside out.

"Papa, will you..."

Hand up, he stopped her, "I will breakfast in my chamber."

She could meet him there, in private, and he would tell her everything. Hopefully the wondering wouldn't keep her awake.

"Very well," she curtsied, "good night then."

He smiled, rather ruefully, "No peck on the cheek?" Which made her smile and comply, her face close enough to hear his whispered, "Lady Grey has gone missing."

She refused to gasp, tucked the lap rope more snugly around her father, "Gone?" she asked ever so softly.

He shrugged. Missing or gone, absconded or of her own free will? It made a difference.

"Shall we?" Lord Whittington held out his arm, which she took as though dressed for court and not in a cape over her nightdress. He smiled approval.

A golden god, quite wonderful really even if his approval felt a tad condescending. It's nice to be appreciated by a man, especially when it would add sauce to Sir Francis' furious glare. Her heart skipped a beat for that darkening scowl.

What was he thinking, to cut up her nicely laid out path?

Really, men could be so difficult.

Chapter 6 ~ Monsters

Eleanor and Whittington barely left the study when Lord Sud-worth lurched toward them.

"Ah, the fair damsel and her prince," he hiccupped and stumbled, landing against the wall. A perfect perch to hold him upright for a deep bow.

"Oh, dear!" Eleanor laughed as a bow transitioned into a slow slide down the wood paneling.

"Good God, Sudworth!" Whittington hurried over to the tangle of his friend, "You can't navigate up from down!"

"Oh, Sshhht.Whitt'n'tn! Goood," hiccup, "fellow in thhe for-eth, brewth hith own," he tapped the side of his nose, "bloody good dwink."

The Earl studied his friend. "I suppose you wish to be helped to bed."

"Poor man, he will suffer," Eleanor sighed. She'd once 'experiment-ed' with her father's libations. A dreadful lesson not to be repeated.

"Came to tell..." Sudworth's bleary eyes lowered.

Whittington nudged him with his toe, "Tell me what?"

Sudworth jolted, then sagged, "What eh?"

Crouching down, Whittington asked, "You came to tell me some-thing?"

"Ah, yeth," the man nodded, "you know, her," he pointed at Eleanor, "thithter, deliful creature, out in the woodth," he slipped fur-ther down the wall, "thent footman after them."

"Was he speaking about Theo?" Eleanor asked.

"Yes," Not in the least amused, Whittington asked, "Them? You sent a footman after them. Who was with Lady Theodora?"

Sudworth blinked, "Your couthin, don't you know. Intheperable."

"Impossible," Eleanor looked about, as if sense stood somewhere to be seen. "Quite impossible."

"I know the fellow in the woods," Whittington told her, "Potent brew, dangerous, truth be told. Don't know if Sudworth was seeing things or if they were in the woods."

"Preposterous!" Eleanor wouldn't have it "Theo would never go out in the woods at night, not without strong, sturdy escort. There are gypsies there."

"No gypsies in my woods," Whittington promised, "so we can eliminate that problem."

Sudworth snuffled, heavy lids shut in sleep.

"Of course not," Lady Eleanor looked toward the floor above, as if she could see Theo snug in her bed. Except she wouldn't be in her bed, she was sharing with Alicia. "You only have ghosts." There had to be a reason people feared ghosts and monsters. Whatever it was, it couldn't be good.

Eleanor took a deep breath, grounding herself. Theo would never venture out in the woods at night. She knew better.

"May I help you get him upright?" she asked, needing something to do, anything rather than run rampant with foolish imaginings.

"No, I think not." Ruefully, Whittington looked down at his inebriated friend. "Movement might just force him to heave. Not pleasant."

Eleanor stepped back, "I hadn't thought of that. Perhaps I'll leave him to you."

"Yes, I'm afraid I have to abandon you. Sudworth certainly needs help," Whittington agreed, "Where are the footmen when they're needed?"

"I'll see to that," she said.

"Wait," he stopped her, "Are you certain those gals haven't gone off on some adventure?"

"Never!" Eleanor told him. They had a firm rule, never, ever, go into the woods alone. "An adventure for Theo would be exploring haberdasheries and milliners. I suspect Miss Alicia is much the same. I'll get those footmen."

WITH EERIE GROANS, spindly tree limbs reached over their heads, creaking, twisting, haunting. Either side of the path, the undergrowth squeaked and rustled, alive at night as it never was during the day.

Arms linked, leaning into each other Theo and Alicia followed the lantern Theo held out in front of them, its light swallowed by the darkness.

"W-w-w-e should go baack," Alicia stuttered, tripped up by fear.

"Yes." Terrified, Theo's breath hitched, but she'd not forget her mission, "We will, as soon as I find Eleanor. We have each other, she's alone!"

"Even if it is her out here, you caaan't stop her," Alicia whispered, "she'll never stop. She'll always find some-some-something."

Theo halted, the lantern swinging in her hand, "It has to be her," she scowled, "why else would her cape and cap be gone?" Conviction strengthened, she switched sides with Alicia, changing hands for the heavy lantern, "We only need to redirect her for now. To get her to stop just for a short time. They will sort it out, once they are married." She tugged Alicia, determined to set off again.

"No," Alicia cried, "I can't, I really, really can't."

"Of course you can, we are perfectly safe. No one will see us."

"Lord Sudworth did," she sniffled.

Alicia rolled her eyes. "Lord Sudworth is past remembering anything."

"Do you think he told Lady Eleanor?" Alicia stumbled forward with Theo's urgent pull only to be stopped again.

"She's not there to tell!" Theo said.

"He said he'd send help."

Theo had forgotten about that, hadn't taken it seriously, "Good. We haven't strayed from the path, they'll find us."

"And what are you missies doin' out 'ere?" Menace boomed in the darkness.

The girls clutched each other, Alicia pulling them back, Theo determined to stand her ground. "Who is that? Where are you?"

A huge hooded figure stepped from behind a tree, standing wide, blocking the path, "I am the monster of these 'ere woods!" He lowered his hood, revealing a misshapen face, parts swollen, others missing, eyes so dark and deep they weren't there at all.

Alicia spun, peeled through the forest, screaming a banshee's cry. The monster cackled to the sky, the sound cut short when Theo's quaking voice demanded, "What have you done with my sister? Where is she?"

THEY WEREN'T IN ALICIA'S room. They were nowhere to be seen.

Eleanor tamped down panic when she'd stood in Alicia's empty bedchamber. The girls could be anywhere. The woods an impossible option. Sudworth was beyond too many cups. He was deliriously drunk.

One step toward Alicia's mother's doorway was all it took before Eleanor regained her equilibrium. No reason to wake the woman. They'd probably gone to her room. Theo would have wanted to check on her.

Except they weren't there, either.

Panic hit, a hard swooping whoosh, freezing her, stealing breath. Sudworth had seen them. He'd sent a footman. The woods were vast.

Something in those woods frightened locals enough to feed fables. There were no such things as ghosts or monsters. But there was such a thing as wickedness. A child's cries, a woman gone missing. A man who didn't exist.

Cloaked in reality, spine rigid with conviction, Eleanor strode out of the hall and straight for the dark woods of her nightmares. If Theo was in the woods she'd have taken the only path she'd known. The one to the lake's edge, where the bear had been found.

Easy to find the path. Following it without aid of light, her own fault. She would manage, she would protect her sister. Eleanor stormed into the dark mouth of the woods when the screams started, shattering the night, waking birds to flight, the undergrowth to rustle and shift with fright and Eleanor to run, cape and nightdress raised to her knees, long strides carrying her down the uneven, root-roughened pathway.

Alicia crashed into her, wild eyed, frantic to get free.

"Where is Theo?" Eleanor demanded, struggling to keep Alicia there, but one violent shove and the girl pushed away, shaking her head, searching for terror over her shoulder before she ran, Eleanor calling after her, "Tell Sir Francis, Lord Whittington! Tell my father!"

Praying the gal heard her, would seek aid, Eleanor pivoted, peering deep into the woods. No monster. No thump of footsteps, pant of exertion. Nothing.

And no Theo.

But there was something in that wood. Oversized and damaged and holding a sister she raised as if her own child. Eleanor kicked off her mules, lifted her skirts and set off, running down the pathway.

Refusing possible threat. She would not allow it.

Nothing would harm her sweet, innocent sister.

Nothing, as long as she had breath to breathe.

Eleanor knew the terror of danger. She would not shy from it now.

Chapter 7 ~ Escape

They found her at the shoreline. A line of torches from the hall to where she stood. All too late.

"What?" Sir Francis reached, to put steadying hands on Eleanor's arms, but didn't dare. Steady logic warred with emotion. Her eyes moving, not seeing, in her own mind, thinking, analyzing. Drained, pale, too fragile to be touched. Comfort would break her.

He stopped Whittington from charging headlong to her aid. Eleanor needed the space not coddling.

"Leave me be," Whittington snapped, "she needs to be shielded."

"She needs to think, Whittington," Sir Francis challenged, "she's coming to grips and searching for solutions."

"That is our job," Whittington countered, "not for a woman..."

"It was a boat!" Eleanor cut him off, head up, eyes now aware, "That's what I couldn't see." Tears pooled and slipped down her cheeks, melting the brittleness Sir Francis so feared. She looked back at the shore, "A boat had been sitting there, upside down, on the bank, damp. I failed to see any significance."

"People fish the lake," Lord Whittington explained, "it's to be expected."

"That one had just come from the lake," she explained, gesturing, "the rower could have found the bear, tossed it on the shore."

"It's not here now," the Earl stood by the flattened grass.

"No, it's just left, look!" Exasperated, she pointed to the drag marks, freshly churned, "He's taken Theo out on the water! What has he done with her?"

"Lady Theodora? Are you certain?" Whittington asked voice gruff with concern.

Eleanor had been standing on the bank, as if she could create a current and pull the whole of it to her. She bent forward, grasped the bottom of her skirt, pulling it up and he realized she was about to walk into the water, as if to chase after her sister. Sir Francis swooped in. She twisted and fought and called him names he didn't even know she knew as he lifted her into his arms. Her nightmare rose to the surface in a shuddering cry she buried in his shoulder.

Redirecting Whittington's glare, he commanded, "Get your men to fan out, be sure Lady Theodora isn't still on this bank."

"She isn't," Eleanor cried, and shoved free, though she didn't leave his side, "I know she isn't."

"We will find her!" Whittington promised, shouting to his men, "I want every tenant, every servant, out here, searching. Every man with a boat, out on the lake!"

He strode off, leaving Sir Francis to care for Lady Eleanor.

"Can you walk?" he dared to ask her, surprised that rather than snap, 'Of course I can walk!' she nodded, wrapping her hand around the upper part of his arm. Uncharacteristically needing his aid. He'd not let her down.

"Where do we go?" she asked him, "What do we do?"

"We go to your father, tell him what has happened." He would have said more but her legs buckled. He lifted her, once more. This time, she did not fight.

"I have you," he whispered, surprised to feel the threat of tears. Such a strong, independent woman, brought to her knees. "Trust the men in this," he told her, "They have the physical prowess. Your task is to let your fears go, so you're free to think."

He headed back to the hall, Eleanor tight in his arms, "I will take care of you."

"YOU CAN LET ME DOWN now," They'd been walking up, through the woods, toward the manor, against the grain of men, young and old, some in livery, some in shirt sleeves, all bearing torches.

Back on her feet, she allowed Sir Francis' arm around her shoulders, offering a strength she desperately needed. Was grateful not to have to ask for it.

"How have they come so quickly?" she wondered, as throngs moved around her.

"The sight of Miss Alicia," Sir Francis explained, "the word went out then. We knew Theo was out here. We didn't know you were there, too."

"You wouldn't have known about the boat, had I not gone."

"True, but an escort wouldn't have hurt," he chastised.

How could she respond to that? There hadn't been time, a weak excuse. She hadn't made it in time, regardless.

"*Let your fears go, so you're free to think.*" Yes, she must. Chasing fear never sent it packing, it just stirred it up into the ugliest brew imaginable. She must be practical.

"This has to do with Tom Baker, Briden's Lake and the Grey's," Eleanor decided.

"Does it?"

This time Eleanor raised an eyebrow. Sir Francis had smiled. "This is not a childish guessing game," she admonished, "this is very serious and I'm very certain!"

Sobered, he murmured "Welcome back," cleared his throat and looked at her, offering his forearm. "Shall we go back to the hall and discuss this with your father?"

Her hand upon his arm, she nodded.

"You are, very possibly, correct," he told her.

"Of course I am," surprised by his agreement despite the facts laid out, "but why do you think so? Because Lady Grey is missing?"

He huffed, "When did he tell... no, don't answer, in the library, when you tucked him in."

"I wouldn't have slept otherwise."

"Not that you will now," he drawled.

The stream of people running to the lake thinned before they finally stepped from the edge of the wood. Its menace remained an ominous shadow hovering over her back. Eleanor doubted she'd feel free of it until they reached the Hall, or that she'd ever be free of it in her dreams.

"We were to leave in the morning," he confessed, "your father was going to request your presence. It seems we have done little this Christmas Season, other than travel."

"We will leave tonight," Eleanor advised.

"I beg your pardon?" Sir Francis asked, "What if they've already found Lady Theo and are, at this moment, returning her to the hall? Do you not want to be here?"

"I would be better placed to finding the root of this horror and ripping it out!" She hadn't meant to sound quite so vicious, but when your own is lost and frightened, well, one does what one must.

SHE'D LEFT LORD WHITTINGTON a missive,

> **Lord Whittington, Papa requires assistance in a matter relating to the missing child, mother and sister. Of the last, I trust she will be safe and in your care by the time you are reading this. If not, then she will be with us, close to Lord Grey's.**
>
> **We will return the moment it is possible.**
>
> **Yours Truly,**
>
> **Lady Eleanor Bayford**

Sir Francis had joined them, of course, as he was the one Lord Grey summoned. Whittington would not be pleased.

"You expect to find her at the Greys'?" Sir Francis asked.

Eleanor thought about it, "No, close but not exactly there."

"But you have a picture, in your mind, of what happened," he said.

"Yes," she nodded, "it's not complete, but yes."

"Hmmmm," he watched her. She watched him.

"Sir Francis, what on earth were you thinking, earlier? Do you say these things to stir trouble?"

Good! Both his eyebrows went up. She'd shocked him from that confounded, patronizing, boredom. It wore off quickly enough, replaced by narrowed eyes as he studied her as intently as he studied evidence.

"Well?" she pushed.

He leaned against the squabs, crossed his arms over his chest. "He'll never understand what drives you."

"And you would?" She sniped.

"Yes," he said, "I would."

"Now, Eleanor," her father intruded, "I've spoken with Sir Francis..."

"Have you? Neither of you have spoken to me and I am here!" The perpetual argument around men, convincing them you were there and intelligent enough to comprehend their conversation. Her father and Sir Francis should be beyond that.

Blunt, even for her, she snapped, "Surely you don't think I would marry you?"

She couldn't, absolutely couldn't marry Sir Francis.

Sir Francis laughed, large and open, utterly unrecognizable. "Not without a fight," he managed to say.

There was no come-back to that. To argue was to offer the fight he suggested. She pinched her lips together, lifted the shade to look out at the passing darkness, and wished the harness bells would clear her thoughts.

"As I told you, Sir Francis, she won't wear it," her father said.

A quick side-glance caught Sir Francis, studying her. "Won't she?"

"The two of you are always at each other's throats," Bayford added, as if he were enjoying himself.

"Fire," was all Sir Francis said, whatever that meant.

She let the flap fall and turned back, refusing to stick to this discussion.

"I don't think we are dealing with murder," she announced.

"Murder?" Bayford asked.

"Yes, Papa, that was the greatest fear, but what if Lady Grey, Lord Thompson and Theo are safe and comfortable?"

Sir Francis sat up straight, leaning forward, eyes narrowed, "You think this possible?"

Attempting nonchalant boredom, Eleanor leaned back against the squabs, or tried to. Attempting to save time, rather than curl and pin and fluff her hair, she'd had Gracie put her in a wig. The fastest option. Unfortunately, the coach ceiling was too low or her wig height too tall. It caught on the ceiling.

"Drat and blast," she murmured, adjusting her hair to her new position.

"Fashion is such a trial these days," her father complained without opening his eyes.

Sir Francis snorted, leaning back again, "You aren't going to tell me."

"Not yet," she said, "It may just be wishful thinking, but I believe them safe, though I haven't a clue where."

"You don't say?" Bayford asked. "And will Lord Grey be part of the search party?"

"Possibly not," Eleanor narrowed her eyes as the two men exchanged glances.

"What aren't you telling me?" She demanded. Both gentlemen remained mute. "What?" she demanded, beyond playing games.

"Lady Grey had been the parson's daughter," her father finally said. "Lord Grey was quite smitten."

"And?"

"Apparently, she was quite smitten with the baker's son. The people of Lower Slough were convinced they were to marry," Sir Francis explained, "until he disappeared."

"One day he was there, the next gone," Lady Eleanor nodded. "I know this much, but not that there was a connection with Lady Grey."

"Lady Grey, Suki back then," her father heaved a sigh, and pulled out his pipe, considered it before putting it back in his pocket, "left shortly after Tom Baker."

"Really?" Eleanor looked at him, "for how long?"

"More to the point," Sir Francis added, "she returned a month after the baby was put on the baker's doorstep."

"Oh," was all Eleanor could say. A babe born, out of wedlock, to Lady Grey and Tom Baker.

"By then, the banns had already been read, for the marriage of Lord Grey and the parson's daughter. Word was put about that she'd been sent away, to his aunt, to learn the ways of a high-born lady."

"Is that why Tom never returned? He'd sent word, that he was in the navy," she said.

"Or so his mother said. We only have her word for it," Sir Francis reminded her.

"While Lady Grey was away, Lord Grey worked very hard to set about destroying Lower Slough," Bayford explained. "He managed it in two years."

"Why didn't you tell me this sooner? This is important," she chastised, "Lord Grey moved Lower Slough to Greystone, removing the old bakery, giving the bakery to another which would send the baker's widow away."

"And anyone connected with Tom," Sir Francis added.

"What do you think he's done with Tom?" Eleanor wondered.

"We don't know. Possibly murder, but there's no body, no proof and his mother claimed to have seen him, shortly before the flooding." Francis offered his grim understanding.

"I knew Lord Grey was the heart of the problem! I just couldn't put it together!" Eleanor shook her head, quickly grabbing her wig.

"Heart of the problem is right," Sir Francis bit out. "He murdered a grandmother and baby, and possibly the baby's father, by flooding them. He knew they were there, we knew it when we investigated, but had no means of proof."

"Are we certain he succeeded?" Lady Eleanor wondered, tapping her fingers on the seat.

This time both men leaned forward. "You sound doubtful," her father said.

"The child crying is Tom Baker's son, the sweet smell you mentioned in the carriage, what I had smelled but failed to consider when we found the bear, was from the baker's widow."

"Not likely," Sir Francis drawled, "Where are they? No one has seen them."

Eleanor heaved a big sigh, murmuring as much to herself as them, "I haven't a clue," she smoothed her lap rug, whispering, "but I pray they are alive and that they have Theo, well and happy and eager to tell us all." Her breath hitched, she blinked back tears. Tears would do no good.

"You think Theo is with them now?" Bayford asked, settling back, more relaxed than he'd been.

"I don't know, Papa, but that is my Christmas wish," she admitted. "That she is perfectly fine. They just don't know what to do with her, lest their secret be revealed."

"Let's hope your wish comes true," Sir Francis nodded.

Eleanor sighed again, mournful even to her ears, "If wishes were horses," she started.

"Beggars would ride." Sir Francis finished for her.

"How does he do it?" she asked, seeing her father settling to sleep.

"You've put my mind at ease," Bayford spoke for himself, quietly, looking every bit like a man sleeping.

"Because I can dream and hope?" Eleanor asked.

"Yes," he nodded, readjusting the pillow between his head and the window, "but you don't stretch your dreams beyond the possible."

But she did. Wishes and horses and all that, there was as much chance something terrible had happened to Theo and the others as there was of wishes becoming reality. Possibly more so.

They all tried to sleep as it was the middle of the night. Eleanor finally gave up, holding her head piece as she shifted.

So quietly, she wasn't certain she was meant to hear him at all, Sir Francis admitted, "Your father may be correct, that your hopes are prompted by something you know, but don't know you know."

"More wishful thinking, a dangerous road."

"I think not," he said, "You are amazing like that."

She couldn't help it, heat rose up her neck, blossoming in her cheeks. Sir Francis was stingy with compliments. When one came, it was inordinately welcomed.

He immediately spoiled her pleasure by saying, "Lord Whittington will forbid your interests, and believe he is doing you a favor."

"Really!" she huffed, "I don't see where it is any of your business."

"We would share pursuits," rather than look at her, he lifted the leather blind, looking out at the cold night.

"We're coming up on the place where the robbers stepped out," he told her.

"Are we?" she remembered, "Theo said you were brilliant in her defense."

Sir Francis chuckled. "It wasn't hard. Coachman and I had both served in the army. And we were prepared. This stretch is notorious."

"Where do they come from?" Eleanor wondered.

"If that was known, they'd be rooted out."

"No doubt." She, too, looked out at the shades of night, wondering if brigands carried torches, to forewarn of their presence. Thoughts like that created false trouble. She dropped the flap, trusting in coachman and the outriders to watch out for them.

"It's snowing," she said, as if he wouldn't have noticed himself.

"And it's Christmas morning, or will be soon. A white Christmas." He pointed out.

What a romantic notion from the cynical, austere Sir Francis. More the sort of thing Lord Whittington would notice. The two worlds apart. Sir Francis serious and droll, Whittington light-hearted and merry. The future Duke laughed easily, making life gayer. Sir Francis' chuckle so often cutting and dark.

It would do Eleanor good to lighten her view of the world in exchange for a dowry.

Besides, Sir Francis was too old.

She slanted a glance, much as she'd done earlier. Again, he watched her.

"I am not that much older than you," he said, anticipating her thoughts.

She looked at her father, head back, mouth open, silently snoring. Asleep.

"You are my father's friend," she said.

"Protégé," he corrected. Her bark of laughter unsettled her father. He closed his mouth, mumbled in sleep and promptly slipped back into his own dreams.

"You disagree?" Francis asked.

"Protégé implies innocence, naiveté," she argued, "if you want to go that route, why not apprentice?"

He tsked his disapproval, "He was once a magistrate, our careers overlapped. That does not make me of an age."

Bayford and Sir Francis were not of an age. But he was considerably older than Lord Whittington.

"Thirteen years," Sir Francis answered before she could ask, "that's the difference between us. I believe your father was ten years your mother's senior."

"How do you know that?" she wondered, "You never met my mother."

"Your father talks of her, did so last night."

"After I went above stairs?"

"Yes," Sir Francis told her, "after you went above stairs."

"Lord Whittington needs my funds," she said, "they've been promised."

"I don't think he'll go without," Sir Francis speculated.

"And you want my skills," she said. There went that infernal eyebrow.

"Is that all I want?" he asked.

"Whatever else could there be?" she asked and refused to be humiliated by any lack of response. She jostled her father, waking him. "I think we are nearing Greystone. This should be interesting."

Chapter 8 ~ Deception

25 *December 1778 – Christmas Day*
Dawn had yet to break as the carriage, its lanterns blazing and bells jingling, pulled into the forecourt of the large stone manor house. Neither sentimentality nor maudlin sorrow prompted Lord Grey's greeting. He was furious. Rigid with it.

The step had yet to be lowered when he stormed toward the rocking conveyance, "First my son and now my wife? Have you not found Tom Baker?" He paced away, hands behind his back, lips pinched tight, eyes dark with lack of sleep.

"Happy Christmas to you," Bayford said, his step crunching on the snow as he stepped down.

"No Happy Christmas here!" Grey challenged. Rightfully so, Eleanor thought, but wondered if the cold hard man ever had a 'happy' anything. But then, she'd not seen him at the best of times. Perhaps he'd been softer before all this.

Doubtful.

"No one has seen that man in four years." Eleanor put her hand in Sir Francis's and made her way out of the carriage. "Why do you think he absconded with your wife and child?"

Nostrils wide, Grey sneered as if she were an interfering gnat. He turned to Sir Francis, "Who else would have done it?" he asked.

"That's what we are here to find out," Sir Francis told him. "For all we know, you are responsible."

Which was the crux of it. Had he murdered the baker's family, his own son and now his wife? Did he have Theo?

How could he have gotten Theo?

Turning purple with rage, Grey exploded, "Me?!"

Eleanor tried to soothe, "It is imperative that we investigate every-one. It is a matter of elimination."

"Tom Baker is alive and here and he did it, that's all you need to know!" Grey raged.

"No one has seen the man," Bayford told him. "Why do you believe he is here?"

"If I had his direction," Grey jabbed at her father, "I wouldn't need you now, would I?"

Eleanor sighed, "Our travels are not done then, are they? We will go speak to the villagers."

"That ungrateful village is full of vicious nattering. Try them, but you won't get the truth. They still blame me, but it was not my fault. Everyone had fair warning. Everyone was told to leave. Can't paint it on me if they didn't."

He stormed into the manor.

Sir Francis watched, "The man summoned me but he's not going to invite us inside?"

"Leave him, shall we?" Eleanor tugged him back toward the car-riage. "If there's room, I'd rather stay at the inn than with that man."

"Looking for a room in an inn on Christmas morning," Bayford mused, "Let us hope we fare better than the baby Jesus."

Sir Francis looked up, "Perhaps we are the three wise ones," he drawled, helping Eleanor into the coach. She hit him with her fan.

"You brought a portmanteau, did you not?" her father asked.

"A valise, yes, but this is my only gown." She looked down at the cream taffeta, so crisp when she put it on, now crinkled and travel worn. Forlorn, she raised her eyes from what she could do nothing about. Sir Francis watched her.

"Handsome," he said.

She snorted, "Not what a lady wants to hear, but I'll take it."

"The dress," he frowned, "not you, you are..."

Head tilted at his hesitation, "Yes, do tell me, what am I?" Amused, Eleanor didn't fault him. Theodora was beautiful, and bright as an angel. Eleanor was not.

"Striking," he nodded his conclusion.

"Better than handsome," Bayford chuckled.

"I meant the dress was handsome," Sir Francis grumbled, "Beauty is a thin veneer easily outshone. Striking encompasses depth..." He spoke to the carriage floor, no doubt embarrassed by his uncharacteristic failure to use words to advantage. "Enough," he lifted the blind, escaping his predicament. "Shall we see where we're going?" and rolled-up the leather flap, closing off the conversation entirely.

"Yes, why don't we?" Eleanor agreed, not at all certain how to digest his words. Had he merely been caught in a corner or did he mean to say her attraction ran deeper than appearances? That he saw beyond pretty, which she was not? Was Whittington capable of as much?

Despite the gloom of the day, the carriage brightened as the sun rose. They rode on in silence along a narrow winding road.

LADY THEODORA WAS MISSING. Presumed abducted. The third person to vanish in almost as many days.

Lord Whittington stood in the entry hall, surrounded by evergreen and holly, pinecones and, he knew, mistletoe above his head. Theo had told him to hang it there, right in the entry hall, for the mischief of catching others unaware.

A delightful young lady, full of innocent merriment, now missing. Presumed abducted. He shivered, looked to the stairs, as if she'd come running down them. Full of stories about Eleanor when all anyone did was watch her.

Untangling Alicia's explanation of where they'd gone and why, took an age. The foolish two had run into the woods, believing Eleanor there, following to bring her back when a huge monster, face twisted and scarred, chased them away.

Alicia fled.

What had the divine Theo done?

Divine?

He shook that off, a figment of fatigue. He was committed to marry Lady Eleanor.

But it was Lady Theodora who was missing. And they must find her.

There had been a moment of hope when Grimms said, "I know the fellow," and led Whittington below stairs, through the kitchens, to confront the baker. A servant who worked alone through the night. Arrived in the kitchens when most were climbing into bed. A man, with a twisted scarred face, who could easily have been in the woods.

They found him there. Tom Shaw, dusted with flour, pulling hot buns from the oven, "Happy Christmas, Grimms," he said over his shoulder, before sliding the pan into the cooling racks, "you're spot on time, they've just come from the oven," he turned, all merriment fleeing at the sight of Lord Whittington. "My lord," he touched his forelock, like a peasant and ducked away, as if Whittington hadn't already witnessed the thick red ropey scars.

"What happened to your face?" the Earl asked.

"Burnt, didn' I," he replied, "bakery accident."

"It's not easy to survive burns like those," Whittington studied him closer, seeing exactly how two, protected, young ladies would see those injuries. "I understand you come through the woods at night, to work here."

"Aye," wary, he looked to Grimms.

"Did you see two young ladies in the woods," Grimms asked.

The baker relaxed, "No, no young ladies," he said.

"When did you arrive?" Whittington looked about, at the full cooling racks.

"Dusk. Earlier than usual. You have guests and it's Christmas." He gestured to dozens of rolls and loaves of bread rising on the sideboard, tall meat pies, shaped like swans and angels. "Honey and fruit cakes are cooling. I will be feeding the Christmas pudding next, so it will flame just right and..."

"You didn't see them?" Whittington asked again.

"No, m'lord, never," the baker claimed, "no one."

The man looked like a monster. It would have been so easy. As they left the kitchens Whittington asked Grimms, "Who would know if he'd gone out?"

"No one, m'lord," Grimms admitted, "but he'd be hard pressed to leave with that much to do before morning."

"For a bit? It wouldn't have taken much time," Whittington suggested.

"Did you see his boots? No mud, no dirt, just flour," Grimms said, "and he's never been a problem. A good man. Gentle."

The answer wasn't at St. Martins. Whittington made his decision. "I will ride to Lord Grey's. See that my mount is readied. And send my valet to my rooms."

"Will you rest first, m'lord?" Grimm asked.

"There's no time, I will leave immediately." He took to the steps, heading for the upper floors, and stopped, "Have a saddlebag prepared, something from the kitchen."

"A bit of brandy, against the cold?" Grimm suggested.

"Precisely, it will be a long ride," he said, "you can inform my father, and the party, that I went to join Lord Bayford. And send word, immediately, if Lady Theodora returns."

He should have left earlier. He was useless here. "I'll take the path around the bottom of the lake." Seldom used, it would be easy to hide evil deeds along that stretch.

He set off through the woods to the trail that led down, around Briden's Lake. The path was far better than he'd expected, but he'd not have to worry about foot pads. The snow was falling, thick and heavy, slow go. No one would be out and about in it.

Not even a monster with a lively young woman.

Worries chased themselves, likes dogs after their own tails, and just as pointless. To break them, he sank into song.

> HARK how all the Welkin rings
> Glory to the King of Kings,
> Peace on Earth, and Mercy mild,
> GOD and Sinners reconcil'd!

Just yesterday, they'd sung that around the pianoforte, Theodora matching him with the sweetest soprano. Perfect blend. Beautifully filling the late afternoon gloom with seasonal joy.

Their audience applauded and bowed and stomped their feet.

A perfect duet.

He could have wept. Stopped, unable to go further, afraid of what he was destined to find. He allowed his mount to drink from the lake, his own breath billowing, like steam, as he searched for peace in the snow, calm in the water.

Please, Lord, this is Christmas, give us Mercy. Lead us to a safe, unharmed, Lady Theodora. Please.

Unlikely. He knew that. If she were to be returned safely, it would have happened. But he'd not stop trying to find her. He'd never stop trying to find her.

Slipping the flask from under his coat, he sipped the spirits, in a shallow attempt at warmth, and waited, wondering if he was casting bad luck to ask for a gift from God on Christmas morning.

Tipping the brandy up, he downed half the flask, corked it, placing it inside his jacket, to keep it warm against his heart. Or, perhaps, to warm his heart. He wasn't certain which.

"Let's go," he said to his mount and started the incline to the top of the ridge.

With the soft fall of snow, he didn't hear the brigands, until they yanked him from the saddle.

Chapter 9 ~ Misadventure of the Worst Sort

"We'll need a private chamber to dine, one with a good fire and some food," Sir Francis told the innkeeper. "We shan't be long above stairs." He looked at Eleanor, prepared for a set-down. Instead, she offered a weary nod.

"Yes sir," the inn keeper promised, "being Christmas day and all, not many stopping. You and your wife can have..." he stopped with Francis' head shake, "Lord Bayford, his daughter and myself. No married couples."

"I see," the man turned to the board holding room keys and grabbed another. "Father and daughter will have adjoining chambers. You will be across from them. Will that suit?"

The three freshened up quickly, meeting below stairs in a small, toasty chamber off the larger public rooms. Anna, the publican's wife, and a serving maid came in with a board full of ham, cheeses, a plate of kippers, bowls of stewed fruit and a heaping basket of breads of all kinds.

"This would tempt a fasting monk." Eleanor sighed.

"Happy Christmas to you," Anna transferred it all to the table.

"Christmas morning," Eleanor murmured, not the least festive. Not without Theo.

"Look at this, Eleanor, buns just like they have at St. Martins Hall," Lord Bayford said, absconding one.

"The raisin-walnut honey buns?" Sir Francis snatched one and a square of spice cake.

"Gluttonous, the pair of you." Eleanor rolled her eyes, asking Anna, "Do you bake them?"

"Oh, no, one of the locals does all our baking, and a tasty job at that." The woman confessed.

Stomach growling, Eleanor put a slice of ham and a bit of cheese on a slab of warm bread, "Oh, my, that is good."

"Just been delivered. Comes fresh daily," Anna crossed her arms, watching them fill their plates. "My Ted will bring you ale. If you aren't needing anything else ..."

Eleanor swallowed, "We will eat then be off, if you could direct us toward Lower Slough?"

Anna stilled, "No longer exists, flooded out. Asides, you don't want to be going that way, nothing there," she looked to the door, "My man will be here in a trice."

"Did you live there, in Lower Slough?" Eleanor pressed.

Sir Francis sighed. The woman flinched every time the town was named.

"Everyone in Greystone here, is from there, moved two year ago."

"Did you know Hannah Baker?"

Anna froze completely, before grabbing up the now empty tray, jabbering away too fast, "That were a long time ago," she said, "and it's Christmas morning. Will you be wanting supper here, or up at the big house?" she asked, "lords and ladies and the like, usually stay at Greystone Manor."

"We will stay and dine here," Lord Bayford said. "No doubt you have the better fare."

"Simple and hearty but it's tasty." Anna curtseyed. "I'll go see to your ale," about through the doorway she stopped, "Christmas goose today, and all sorts. Hadn't expected guests, but we've enough. Plum pudding for the end. You'll enjoy it." And she darted away.

The serving gal did not follow. "You're here for Lord Grey?" she asked, "Cuz' Mam and Pap are good patrons. They pay their rent, they have clean rooms and good food and the beer is the best in the county. Pap has helped searching for the lad and his mum after that. That's all we knows, no more..."

"But do you know the path to Lower Slough?" Sir Francis asked, spreading jam on a slab of bread.

"All grown over, ne'r be able to walk in this snow."

"Then we shan't go that way, shall we?" Francis said, kicking Eleanor's foot under the table. She jerked her head up, glared at him, but didn't counter. In fact, she added, "No, I suppose not, though I'd heard the view from the ridge is spectacular."

That's Eleanor, heavy handed but quick to adjust. The serving girl relaxed, "Oh, aye, that it is, but you'll have to go by horse. Carriage would never make it."

Bayford stayed at the inn, in case word came from St. Martins. Eleanor and Sir Francis obtained a mount from a stable lad, young boy who only dared let them have old Bess, a broad backed mare. "Only the ostler can let you have the fine stallions, and he's not here account of Christmas and all."

"I'll ride behind," she told the lad, which had been easy up to the ridge, where the view proved to be as magnificent as claimed. After that, they went downhill, into woods, hindering sight of anything but trees and forcing Eleanor to slide from the croup to the back of the horse and against Sir Francis. Their faces so close, when he turned and asked, "What are you looking for?" her nose brushed his cheek.

"A house, home." Eye-to-eye, she couldn't miss the flicker of something unidentifiable. Fortunately, he turned back as she continued, "Smoke from a chimney? The sound of the child? The scent of cooking." She looked up, at the sky. No smoke.

Arms around him, for security, she decided she was perfectly safe and pulled back. He pressed down, holding her in place. "It's warmer this way," he claimed.

The problem was, she liked it. Liked the spicy smell of him, the heat of him. Too much. Before he could stop her, she pulled free, putting her arms between his back and her stomach.

"Why do you think Theo is here? They searched the area, reached it by boat, no one saw any sign," he challenged.

"They had enough time to get over to the other shore, and away. There was a splash of oars, perhaps even a grunt, but I can't be certain. By the time I was thinking, everyone was there surrounding me, noisy."

"There's more to it than that," he said, not asked. Said.

She chuckled. He did know her well.

"Of course there is more. There was the scent of baking when we found the bear. And there was the crying and, later laughter. One child, then two! And the baking." She pushed away, bracing her arms on his back, deciding distance helped her think. "That was the one thing that made me question the death of the child and his nana."

"Baking?" Sir Francis reached back and pulled her arms around him, "You'll freeze."

He had a point. It was cold. A layer of snow covered them, their breaths rising in the air.

Back in the warmth, she shamelessly snuggled, so comfortable with this man, she didn't think not to.

"Tell me," he'd gone all gruff, getting her back to business, "why the baking?"

"Hannah Baker was a baker, and from all accounts a very good one. Who else produced those heavenly scents?"

"The scent could have come from the Hall."

Eleanor laughed, "You saw, when we were on the ridge, Lower Slough was built in a deep valley, that's why it was such a perfect place for the lake. The banks rise up on either side. How would the scent carry up and then down, into the valley? It was coming from inside the valley."

"The far side?" he frowned back at her, "The ridge is high and steep."

"Sandstone," she told him, "most of the land around here is sandstone." Embarrassed she admitted, "I read about the lands, to learn before coming here. If I was to be the countess..."

"Duchess..." he corrected.

"Countess as long as his father is alive," she told him, "then I should know about the land, it's profits, it's strengths and weaknesses."

"You studied about the Summerton estates?" he was incredulous.

She sniffed her disdain, "And well I should, especially as it is so horribly in debt."

He nodded. "Explain the sandstone."

"You won't believe me, nobody knows about them but Papa. He took me there, once, and swore me to secrecy."

"You're going to tell me about those little houses built into the sandstone."

"Yes! You know!" she crowed, "Totally hidden, but they have everything you need. We haven't a clue who lived there or when, but they were delightful."

"And you think there are some here?" He stopped, his nose twitching.

"Yes," Eleanor whispered, "I think they are here, and by the scent, we are very close to the chimney pot!" Sure enough, they rounded the bend to find a squat tree stump with smoke coming from it. A wonderful disguise.

What wasn't disguised was the huge man standing in the path, his hood up, almost covering a misshapen face.

"You'll be wanting your sister," he said and turned around, walking away.

Startled, they stared after him until Eleanor kicked old Bess, "Go!" she told the slow-moving beast, "don't lose him!"

IT WAS A LITTLE HOB of a house, no more than a doorway in a stone wall. Eleanor had to duck to get that ludicrous head piece under the lintel. Sir Francis had to duck himself, worried about standing once inside, but that was not a problem.

The whitewashed room must have had ten people in it, a dozen including them, fitting without having to stand cheek to jowl. Lanterns hung from a high ceiling that curved gradually down to become the walls, a huge wide arch. Bright and warm, the fireplace wide and deep with baking ovens on either side. Doorways led to rooms beyond, but no telling if they were for storage or sleeping or anything else. This home, hidden by evergreens and undergrowth, far grander than any tenant structure.

And it was warm, blessedly warm after their ride through the snow, but he'd go back to that ride, with Eleanor's arms around him. Blessed fire that was.

It didn't take long for the sisters to spot each other.

"E!" Theo charged across the room, would have tumbled them both, if he hadn't caught the mass of them, hugging, crying, delighted to be found, to find. A healthy chuckle rose, and he joined their joy.

They'd found Theo.

Or they'd been found. Impossible to do the finding without help. The damaged face looked familiar, but he wasn't certain, the size a bit off. Out of courtesy, he'd not looked closely at the baker from St. Martins but how many men had this sort of facial scar? Amazing he was even alive.

A lad of about five, curly furred toy bear in his arm, leant against an old woman, who sat at the fireside end of a long table. Beside her, looking younger than she had the morning before, sat Lady Grey, Lord Thompson asleep in her lap, his arm in a sling, with a toy bear's nose peeking out.

He'd believed them dead, gone to flood and misadventure. Never expected to find them alive.

Yet here they were. Even the grandmother.

Tears glistened in Eleanor's eyes, though she'd never doubted the possibility.

Miracles, stuff of the imagination, yet they'd found a heart full on Christmas day. More than anyone could ask for, yet he prayed, despite his cynical heart, that he too could reap such a thing. Another Christmas miracle, this one for him, when so many had already been granted.

Sir Francis nodded toward the towheaded boy and the older woman, "Hannah and Briden Baker, I presume," he said, "and you are St. Martin's baker, Tom Baker?" He confronted the giant of a man with the damaged face.

"No," the man said, "theys call me Bart, that there be Tom Baker," and pointed toward one of the doorways now open, another standing there with the same sort of injuries.

"He's known as Tom Shaw these days," Lady Grey explained, as he came up to stand behind her, a hand on her shoulder, "He knew better than to come into the area as himself."

"And the rest?" Sir Francis asked.

Lady Grey looked to Hannah, who nodded saying, "It's time to stop hiding. Grey's too dangerous, he must be stopped and too many know, now, where we are."

Theodora pushed away from Eleanor and ran to the woman, knelt at her side, "It's my fault! I am so sorry, but we won't tell anyone, no one! I promise! We can keep your secret!"

"Get him," Hannah nodded at one of the younger men, "it's time." And she sighed, as if a heavy burden lifted from her shoulders only to be replaced by the hang-man's noose.

"I KNEW YOU WERE HERE," Eleanor told the older woman, "it was the baking, the sweet scent of it, the heavenly taste. Nothing like this anywhere and suddenly, in two closely related communities. Mother and son, the only explanation." She took a seat, "May I?"

"Oh, E, they are so good and have faced the worst ordeal!" Theo gushed. "And I've spoiled it all."

"We thought you were dead," Eleanor chastised, blunt as ever.

"But I'm not!" Theo smiled, "I've been safe as houses."

"Houses t'wernt safe in Lower Slough," someone snorted.

Theo, with all her enthusiasm, probably had created trouble. But she was safe, now plunked down next to Eleanor, holding her hand in both of hers.

"I told them all you would figure it out, E! I told them you would know it all," Theo claimed, "and help them solve the tangle they face."

"Parts of it, yes," Eleanor admitted. "I know parts."

"Tell us then, Lady Eleanor," the old lady said.

But she was interrupted as the door burst open and Lord Whittington was shoved through the opening, followed by two men.

"Whittington!" Theo gasped, "you are here as well?"

"You were lost," he said. "Dear Lord, you were lost!"

Chair toppling, Theo rushed to him, grabbing his cape, "You've come to no harm?" enthusiasm exchanged for a hoarse whisper. Whittington swallowed, took her hands, removed them from his cape front, nodding as he very deliberately looked to Eleanor and bowed, "My Lady."

"Right prat," Sir Francis murmured. Eleanor tried not to laugh.

"You don't have to martyr yourself, Whittington," he barked, "For god's sake, let her know you want the other sister, and free us all!"

The spit of the fire, the rustle of a dog the only sounds, until Eleanor's chair legs scraped the flagstone floor, as she stood. "Shall we get on with sorting out what is here?" she asked.

Theo bit her lip, studied the floor, inched away from Whittington, deflating with each moment. Whittington stood, a failed soldier, prepared for punishment, no matter how onerous.

"Oh, E," Theo started, "he's perfect for you."

Eleanor rolled her eyes. "A moment ago, you admitted to creating an upset for these people, do you want to sort it out or not?"

"Yes," Theo looked up, "I am nothing but a troublesome creature."

"Yes, you are," Eleanor agreed, "but good can come from trouble, so please, be seated so these gentlemen may sit as well." She waited, for others to take their places. Sir Francis leaned against a wall. Whittington kept close to the door. To seek escape? Possibly, but she wasn't concerned about him.

Unfortunately, she was not often concerned about him.

He may look grim to the others, but Eleanor spotted the sparkle in Sir Francis' eyes. Ever so slightly, he dipped his head, urging her to continue. She smiled in return.

"What has Lord Grey done, to threaten you?"

"A threat and more!" Tom Baker bit out and his eyes filled with tears, "He's tried to kill my boys!"

Lady Grey reached up, knuckles white, clasping Tom's hand on her shoulder.

Eleanor pressed her lips tight, clarifying thoughts, "Let us start at the beginning. He attempted to flood, and drown, your mother and son. You managed to get them here, to these," she gestured, not knowing what to call them, "caves?" she asked, "Were these always here? Or did you carve them out? Was that where you disappeared to?"

"Here for donkey's years," Hannah said, "only a few knew of them. Afraid the kids would get lost in them. They go deep inside the cliff, so we stayed mum. All of us, who had a reason to fear Grey."

"Suki helped Mama," Tom squeezed Lady Grey's shoulder. "She knew he planned to flood the town early, barely had time to warn everyone."

"Did anyone see or hear him order the opening?"

"Howie, over there." Hannah motioned to one of the young boys, "soon as we knew, he kept watch, saw him order the man to open the dam."

Sir Francis told them, "We looked for the man who actually opened the flood gates. Apparently, he moved on."

"Grey pushed him, right in," Howie bit out.

"Good god!" Whittington murmured, "Threw him over?"

"Were you here, Tom?" Eleanor asked, "Or did you really go, as everyone thought."

"Gang pressed into the navy, wasn't I? Never even seen the sea, didn't know anything about it. I think he meant to have me thrown overboard at some point, but they weren't about to give up a decent cook."

"Heaven it was," said Bart, the other man with burn scars, "until the ship blew, sending men and burning timbers flying through the air. T'wert the sea salt that saved us and God. N'un else made it. Just us, left for dead, hugging a bit of flanking, floating in t'a water so long they had to pry our arms from the timber. Doc said if not for tha', we'd be goners for sure."

"You were in the navy with him."

"Aye, survive agether and come 'ere. I wer't goin' on, but no wer't to go. Here t'wer good 'nuff fur me."

"Grey's brought the pressing gangs back," Hannah said, "Hoping to get Tom again. They've been stopping carriages, pulling fellows out."

"Our robbers!" Theo gasped.

"Because he knows Tom has returned?" Eleanor asked.

"Aye. He knows," Tom answered, Suki finishing, "Last week, Grey started acting odd, but I didn't know why, didn't dare question him. He could be violent.

"Then Thompson went missing," she sniffed, Tom started to finish for her but she stopped him, caressed her son's head before covering his ears, "he," she stopped, waited and tried again. It took four goes before she managed, "Grey took him to the well, by the old chapel, lifted the lid, dropped him in and shut it!"

She held her boy, rocking, weeping.

"Good God!" Whittington said.

"You saw this?" Sir Francis asked, "You witnessed it?"

"No," she shook her head, "one of the grounds-men saw it. A good thing Tom taught the boys to swim,"

"Course I did. Life and death," he said.

Suki continued, "There were hand holds, down the inside of the well, but he's just a toddler, he'd never have managed them, and the lid was closed, so no one would have heard his cries." She couldn't continue.

"The groundsman got him out?" Eleanor asked.

"Aye, and knew better than to return him home," Tom said, "so he took him over to St. Martins."

"That's why we found the toy!" Eleanor exclaimed.

"He dropped it. Cried and cried, but they couldn't go back. You were all there and he was cold." Lady Grey explained.

"He's safe now," Tom soothed, "the man can't harm him now."

"Why did he do it?" Eleanor asked, "Had he seen you and..."

"In the woods, he saw us, the boys playing," Tom explained, "When you came with the toy, that should have been in the well, he confronted Suki. We all feared he'd kill her next."

Suki laughed, "He tried." She looked at Lady Eleanor and Sir Francis, "After you left yesterday morning, he said Thompson wasn't his son, would never inherit from him, and locked me in my rooms. He told the servants he was afraid I'd do myself a mischief, because Thompson was missing, so I climbed out a window."

"Now everyone knows we're here," Hannah said, rising, "We'll have to move, all of us, find somewhere else."

"Do you?" Eleanor asked. "Lord Grey has committed crimes."

"Impossible!" Lady Grey exclaimed, "Our word over his? He's an earl. He's told me I would never win."

"Shushhhhhh," Tom eased, "let this lady speak."

"You don't have to hide anymore," Sir Francis said, "Come to the Greystone Village Inn. Join us for Christmas supper."

"And have Lord Grey swoop us up? Don' think so," one man groused, to the agreement of all.

"You will be under my protection," Whittington promised.

"And mine," Sir Francis said. "I am, after all, magistrate for the districts. And Lord Bayford holds power."

"As does my father, the Duke of Summerton. That's the consequence of two magistrates, two earls and a duke to Lord Grey."

"Don't know," Bart shook his head, "we wert safe here 'cuz no ones knew about us."

"Well, we know now, and we intend to help," Eleanor told them, turning to Sir Francis. "Are you prepared to have me at your back for the return to Greystone? Theo may ride with Whittington. No doubt his horse is not quite as sturdy as ours and will be pleased with the lighter weight."

She watched the infinitesimal twitch of Sir Francis' lip. She'd almost made him laugh.

Weighted down by guilty hearts, Whittington and Theo looked miserable. Theo would never be so cruel as to betray her sister in deed. She'd not do so in heart, either, but hearts have a way of tugging us where we'd rather not go.

Sometimes, one must turn away from the heart's command. Sometimes, when we are very, very fortunate it will lead us to the possible inside the impossible.

This Christmas demanded miracles all around and it was her turn to work them. If she could. If wishes were horses.... but wishes were flimsy things.

She was not.

She would find solutions.

She would.

Except their mount maneuvered a decline, sliding her against Sir Francis' back.

Pragmatic to the core, finding clear logic in the muddiest of times, her mind dissolved. A puddle of mush when she dearly needed to think ... and would, in a moment.

Lady Eleanor closed her eyes, defied a lifetime of practicality, and nestled closer.

Chapter 10 ~ Making the Impossible Possible

S ir Francis and Eleanor arrived first, handing their mount over to the ostler.

"Yous went there, where we's told you not to," he groused.

"Magnificent view," Eleanor called over her shoulder as she walked to the inn. Sir Francis chuckled behind her, "Yes, superb view. Highly recommended."

She turned back as she opened the door, and caught him at it again, looking at her. Rather pleased with herself, she lifted her chin. Perhaps there was a man who would want her person when she'd always thought they'd merely want her funds. If she were lucky, her mind, but she'd never thought to command physical interest.

Apparently, she'd been wrong.

A little thrill wiggled through her.

"Pleased with yourself?" Sir Francis reached around to hold the door she'd opened.

"Yes," she told him, stepping over the threshold, "I am."

"So you should be."

They found Bayford in their small antechamber, a cup of tea before him. "We have a bit of work to do, Papa, and not much time to do it."

"You've found Theodora?" he asked.

"We have. She will be arriving shortly with Lord Whittington," Eleanor beamed.

Bayford looked from his daughter to Sir Francis and back again, "I sent him the wrong daughter, eh?" He sighed, bowing his head, "I did so want you to form a good marriage. One where you could be comfortable."

"I am not without means, Lord Bayford, and there is no other man who can appreciate your daughter as I have and will." Sir Francis challenged.

Bayford waved his words away, "Yes, yes, I know that. I've seen your interest in her growing through the years, but let me be frank," eyes narrowed, he looked him straight, "you two bicker all the time, too much. Our Eleanor has enough seriousness, she needs light in her life. With Theo caught in marriage and children, who will give her that? Certainly not you!"

Eleanor laughed, startling them both, "I will still have Theo in my life, and her husband and, God willing, children of my own, but Papa, Sir Francis and I do not bicker, we debate, and both thoroughly enjoy it!" she claimed, "And there is more laughter in Sir Francis than you would suspect. He's just subtle with it."

He wasn't laughing now, his eyes were hot and serious and focused on her, only her.

"I want him for my husband, and that is that!" she demanded.

"I see," her father said into his kerchief. He wasn't coughing. That was a chuckle he hid.

"Well then, as that's settled, you'd best tell Whittington and Theodora because they are positively wretched!" Eleanor ordered, assured it would be as she dictated. Not even her father countered her when she was firm.

But no one had to tell them, for they were standing in the doorway, had been for some time. Eleanor and Sir Francis so caught in their own defense they'd failed to notice them.

Lord Bayford hadn't, "Are you happy with this, you two, or do I need to pry..." Theo flung herself across the room to hug her father, cutting off whatever he meant to say.

"Oh, Father! You have made me so happy!"

Whittington, too, stepped forward with alacrity, "If it pleases you, Lord Balford, I know the funds are attached to your eldest daughter, as they should be. But I would like to marry Lady Theodora. We will make ends meet, in all and any ways needed."

"Eleanor will get the majority of the funds," Bayford said.

Whittington swallowed, but did not shy from reality, "We will deal as we must."

"Papa," Eleanor warned, with her sternest voice. Sir Francis guffawed.

Lord Bayford nodded, trying not to smile, "We will see what we can do," he told them.

"Good," Eleanor said, "because we have some very important business to discuss. We have a Lord to be condemned and a family to free."

Chapter 11 ~ All Bad Things Must Come to an End

They were not a merry troupe. Scraggily and morose, the Bakers and their community arrived, warily looking about them, expecting strong arms and prison chains. Yet they brought their Christmas fare, to mesh with what Greystone Inn provided. The innkeeper and his wife, their daughter and son, were not to be found once the others stepped in.

All awaiting Grey's wrath.

And Grey joined them, no doubt of that. Before he knew what was what, Lord Bayford had invited him. Carriage bells jangled, forewarning his arrival, the coach barely visible through the steam of the windows.

A scrappy young lad charged for the door, boldened by the move, others followed. Sir Francis anticipating the risk, had coachman and outriders ready to block the way.

"We'll not have you come to harm," Bayford promised.

"That why he's comin'" Tom said, stoic for himself. He'd not brought Lady Grey, or the boys, though Hannah stood there, resolved to see this through, no matter the consequence.

"We can't live in hiding for the rest of our lives," she told those trying to leave, "Hear them out."

"Not with Grey," another shook his head, "I'll not..."

The door from the kitchen opened. "Careful, damn you!" bellowed the Duke of Summerton, to Grimms, "You'll do me a damage!"

"Father," Lord Whittington bowed to his father, "I pray you had a good journey."

The Duke snorted, "On snow covered roads, missed my Christmas dinner. Goose! First good meal since this damnable foot," he grumbled, but lost his ire when he spotted his old friend, "You said you needed my consequence," he said to Bayford, "and you shall have it."

"Many thanks, your Grace," Bayford bowed.

To his son, he added, "Our house party seems to be managing just fine without us. Word is Miss Giles and Lord Sudworth may make a match of it."

"Really? Sudsy's getting leg shackled?" Whittington winked at Theo who beamed, "Many a surprise this Christmas."

"That's not Lady Eleanor." He scowled at his son, "What is this about?" He wheeled himself forward as Lord Grey pushed into the room.

The door hit the Duke's gout ridden foot and chaos erupted. The Duke bellowed and cursed in language unfit for mixed company. Spotting Tom Baker, Lord Grey barged past the Duke, tripping over his foot, using the man's aching leg to right himself, ignoring the screams of pain and profanities.

Up again, Grey launched for the carving knife sitting upon the board, awaiting the Christmas goose. Once in hand he charged around the table, fighting to get to Tom, all the while shouting, "I knew you were here you... I'll kill you this time, I will!"

Coachman and the outriders had been fighting an exodus of the Baker community before hearing Sir Francis shout above the melee, "Stop Lord Grey!" They did.

By the time it was over, the only people left from the hidden community were Tom, Hannah and Bart. They never tried to leave. Tom didn't run from the threat of the knife, though he'd pushed his mother behind him.

"Murderous sort, your Grace," Bayford said, flicking a hand at Grey.

"Your Grace?" Face mottled with rage, struggling against the confining hold, Grey scanned the room, finally recognizing the man in the wheeled chair. The man he'd so discomposed. "See here, your Grace, this man should not be here. He's a criminal, the worst sort and his mother why, they kidnap children and..."

"If you will pardon me, your Grace," Grimms said, from where he was crouched beside the Duke, adjusting the foot of his chair, seeing to his comfort, "the man Lord Grey is referring to is your baker."

"My baker?" the Duke of Summerton asked, "The one who creates those divine marvels? The one I want up in London?"

"Yes, your Grace," Grimms rose, backing away, bowing.

"You'll not have my baker," Summerton told Grey.

"He's dangerous," Grey said, "not safe to sleep at night..."

"Grimms?" Summerton asked his butler.

"He has the run of St. Martins at night, your Grace. No one else awake then, when he works. Yet nothing's gone missing, no misconduct of any sort. All safe in their beds."

"Helpful," Bayford nodded, "but there is more."

"Tell us then, as the scent of Christmas dinner beckons," Summerton said.

"The Earl of Grey is responsible for one murder and the attempt of a number more," Sir Francis explained. "We have witnesses and people in fear for their lives. As he will not be tried in a court of mine, Lord Bayford thought it best you were aware of the situation, so you could join him in addressing the House of Lords."

"I see," Summerton scoured Grey with a glance, "I see. Murder? Who has he attempted to murder?"

"His son for one, pulled from a well he dropped him down, your Grace." Eleanor told him.

"Lady Eleanor," the Duke pointed at her, "at last."

"It is, your Grace," Eleanor curtseyed.

"You would make a fine duchess," he said.

"That is most unfortunate, as I won't be marrying your son. Though I do promise to give my sister instruction."

"See here! Bayford! We had an agreement! Whittington!" Summerton blustered, "What is this world coming to?"

"Equal agreement, just a different daughter, your Grace," Bayford smiled, rather enjoying himself. "Lady Eleanor will not have it any other way."

"Can't you control your own gals? God's sake man," he grumbled.

"Ha!" Bayford said, "Never have, never will. They're smarter than me." And everyone laughed but Hannah, who realized one of the reasons the Duke was so unhappy.

"You've pain of the foot, but I am thinking you have an empty stomach as well," she worked her way past everyone and to the kitchen door, "Anna, time for the meal. Tell Ted we need a secure place to hold Lord Grey, so he can't escape."

"I'll guard the door," Bart offered.

"No need," Coachman said, "there's a place in the stable he'll not be able to get free of."

"I'm an earl!" Earl Grey cried.

"You bought that title!" Summerton charged, "You've been an earl for a spit of time. No history, no alliances. You took advantage of a long-titled family's lack of heirs and whisked their title and lands away. I doubt that will hold much stead in the House," he shook his head, as they dragged Grey out, "and don't let him near my foot!"

"Thank you, your Grace," Sir Francis bowed.

"I trust you will give me the full facts, but that gal is right. Let's get that goose out here!" he leaned over to the Earl of Bayford, "Doctor had me on a god-awful regime, flushing the kidneys. Near starved me."

"There will be commoners at the table, your Grace," Bayford warned.

Bayford looked over at the odd assortment of guests coming to sit, "It doesn't rub off, does it? In younger days I frequented dens of commoners. Amusing times. Just tell them beware. I'll have them hung if they kick my foot." He looked over his shoulder, "Grimms?"

"I will sup in the kitchen, your Grace," he said.

"Just as well," Summerton said, "Can't have you getting too high in the in-step."

Grimms actually smiled.

26th December 1778 ~ Boxing Day ~ The 2nd Day of Christmas

It had been a high-spirited Christmas table, festivities lasting well into the night. Lives freed, dreams realized. Even Lady Grey attended, having been waiting with the boys in a room above stairs.

Sir Francis considered the long line of folks eager to speak of Grey's evil doings, to release the poison of the man. But not a one spoke of the hidden homes, preferring to keep that secret. And well they should.

The children danced and played about the room, never once going near the Duke's foot. Remarkably well behaved for brats. Perhaps he'd have some, one day. He'd never thought of it. Until now.

He had to know but didn't know how to ask. Did Eleanor *want* to marry him, or was she merely easing her sister's guilt?

He did not want to be a martyr's choice. He wanted inside her heart.

Except he and Eleanor did not speak the language of romance. He didn't possess the words. His heart fed on her practical nature, her brilliance, waiting for her to see him, not as her father's peer but as her life's partner.

And then her father got it in his head that she would be the Duchess of Summerton. A duchess. She was perfect for the role. None finer. Except Whittington was not right for her. He would have tried, they would be friendly to each other, but their lives would follow different paths. She would be lonely.

"What are you thinking," she asked, right there beside him.

"Where did you come from?" He'd been outside, standing in the courtyard, watching as the coach was readied for their departure. They would travel home today.

"Papa is getting ready and I thought it best to leave Theodora and Whittington to their breakfast. Neither is comfortable when I am about. I can't seem to convince them..."

"Marry me," he cut her off, without daring to look at her. *"Surely you don't think I would marry you?"* she'd said. Then defended him yesterday. Had she done it for them, or for Theo?

Anything for Theo. Eleanor would give up her life for her sister. That included marrying him. He didn't want to be Theo's happiness. He wanted to be Eleanor's world.

"Marry me and I will allow you freedom to be you. We will be more than husband and wife, we will be helpmates, partners."

Out of the corner of his eye, he saw her remove her glove and flick something from her face. With the slightest of movements, he turned his head, just enough to catch her placing the backs of her fingers to her cheeks.

"You're blushing," he faced her full now. Lady Eleanor was no blushing ingénue. She was a woman of science, strong minded and strong willed.

"Yes," she looked at him with wonder, "I rather think I am."

"Did I embarrass you?" he asked.

She swallowed and looked about.

"What?" he asked.

Taking his hand, she headed up the path to the inn door, babbling, which Eleanor never did, "Impossible to imagine anyone would want me to be anything different than I am, and yet the world is so full of expectations, one never knows which one to listen to and which one to ignore and," she stopped, under the trellis, near the door and took a breath, as though she'd been running.

He waited. She pointed above their heads. Mistletoe.

"I see," he drawled and leaned over touching his lips on hers.

The second day of Christmas and he'd received his gift.

"Happy Christmas, Lady Eleanor," he murmured, "I gift you my heart," he said, wishing he could offer prettier words.

"Happy Christmas, Sir Francis," the brightness of her smile, the rosy red of her cheeks bringing tears to his eyes, "I accept your gift and return it in kind."

Behind them, her father coughed, "I always said, this was to be your Christmas, Eleanor. I see that it is."

And it was, for two sparkling couples, celebrating their love, announcing betrothals beneath the mistletoe on the second day of Christmas.

To a Bright and Merry Christmas ~
Of the heart, for the heart
Becca St. John

Don't miss out!

Visit the website below and you can sign up to receive emails whenever Becca St. John publishes a new book. There's no charge and no obligation.

https://books2read.com/r/B-A-HUQG-JNIV

BOOKS 2 READ

Connecting independent readers to independent writers.

Did you love *Lady Eleanor's Christmas*? Then you should read *Summerton*[1] by Becca St. John!

[2]

*He married for money, she wed by force ~ Neither considered love part of the bargain*On the brink of losing everything, the Duke of Summerton marries heiress Caroline Howlett, but at what cost? She wants neither his crumbling estate nor his title, and what is he, as a man, without them? Before he can resolve this dilemma, something more dangerous than doubt threatens their marriage.When Caroline said she'd rather be dead than married to the duke, she hadn't meant it literally. Forced into marriage by her guardian, Caroline doesn't give a fig for the idle life of the aristocracy. She wants to run her father's enterprises, and she will, once dead bodies stop getting in the way.Aided by Summerton's widowed aunt, amateur sleuth Lady Eleanor, the duke and his re-

1. https://books2read.com/u/mYoeKG

2. https://books2read.com/u/mYoeKG

luctant bride scramble to discover just who is trying to kill them. **The Lady Eleanor Mystery ~ Regency romantic mystery with a touch of Gothic.**

Read more at https://www.beccastjohn.com/.

Also by Becca St. John

Lady Eleanor Mysteries
Summerton
The Gatehouse
Lady Eleanor's Christmas

The Handfasting Series
Seonaid
The Reah

Women of the Woods
The Healer
The Protector
An Independent Miss

Watch for more at https://www.beccastjohn.com/.

About the Author

Writing was a tool, not a toy, until a stay in a haunted hotel and a bookcase full of dog-eared romances. Hooked, Becca read old romances, new romances, both sexy and sweet, until her own tales begged to be written.

Living in Florida, Becca divides her time between dreaming up stories, diving deep into history, kayaking, and swimming. Her husband gives her the space she needs by fishing in the mangroves and waterways or watching football (the English sort) with his British buddies. Becca and her hubby break the routine with adventure travel; though, at heart, Becca is a homebody believing there is no greater playground than inside the mind.

Read more at https://www.beccastjohn.com/.

www.ingramcontent.com/pod-product-compliance
Lightning Source LLC
Chambersburg PA
CBHW030543130626
46552CB00006B/2402